NECK-ROMANCER BOOK TWO

NECK-ROLOGICAL

ELIZABETH DUNLAP

This is a work of fiction. Names, characters, places, and incidents either are the product of the author's imagination or are used fictitiously, and any resemblance to any persons, living or dead, business establishments, events, or locales is entirely coincidental.

NECK-ROLOGICAL

Copyright © 2020 by Elizabeth Dunlap

All rights reserved.

Cover Art by Pixie Covers; Edited by Pixie Covers

This book is protected under the copyright laws of the United States of America. Any reproduction or other unauthorized use of the material or artwork herein is prohibited without the express written permission of the author.

First Printing: Aug, 2020

Printed in the United States of America

First Edition: Aug, 2020

❦ Created with Vellum

Dedicated to the Mischievous Bitches.
I could not have gotten through this year without your love, support, and inappropriate memes.

P.S. Spoopy is not a typo.

DISCLAIMER

For Adult Audiences 18+.
Language and actions may be deemed offensive to some.
Sexually explicit content.

This series includes pregnancy, and M/M relationships, men loving other men. Considering how thirsty Alec is for literally everyone in Jaz's harem, we are not surprised at all.

Trigger warnings: Death.

I

THE CLAUS MANSION

Goddess, I know I said I'd try to stop being a whiny loser, but here we are.

Of course, I was not the only whiny loser in the Claus mansion, as there was a certain mussy haired warlock I hadn't seen in a week. I peeked an eye open from my spot in the parlor, glaring at the ceiling where I knew Alec's room had to be.

Goddess, you sent me three soulmates, and one of them is a total asshat. Kinda feel like that's on you.

I felt as miserable as an expired coupon.

Alec was off pouting, or *whatever* Diva Pants had been up to lately. Gilbert was spending most of his time in the attic because he said the Claus mansion '*felt weird.*' And then there was Pierce, who could barely shift out of his wolf form for fear of being exposed by the estate staff. He wasn't even here right now, having once again disappeared into the forest beside the mansion, leaving me by myself, *asshole*.

So that brought us here, where I was attempting my morning meditation while trying *not* to think about how all three of my soulmates were absolute cunt waffles.

When that thought wasn't there, I just felt hollow and empty. I couldn't shake my despair over being unable to resurrect that centaur at the school dance. My epic failure sat there in front of me, like a giant zit on the end of my nose.

My phone buzzed where it sat on the rug next to me. My parents were relentless in their attempt to make me answer their calls. After telling them I was spending a few weeks at Alec's family home, I assumed they would let me relax and recover without being disturbed, but alas, it was not to be.

Defeated, and feeling a little lonely, I picked my phone up and answered it.

"Jasmine Sofia Neck, just *what* on *god's green earth* do you think you're doing?" My mother's shrill '*I'm about to set the house on fire*' voice was deafening, and I held the phone away from my ear until she was finished ranting.

I bit back a snarky response that would just earn more yelling in my ear. "I'm meditating."

She clicked her tongue at me, and I hoped our house wasn't already ablaze from her wrath. "Don't you use that tone with me, Jasmine. You know exactly what I mean. I was fine with you disappearing to the Claus estate, especially after finding out that the Claus heir is one of your soulmates, but I did not agree to you ignoring my calls and keeping me in the dark on your condition."

Condition? It wasn't like I was ill. Or pregnant. My head shook to knock that thought loose, because NO. I was barely old enough to drink, having a child was not on my list of things to do. Besides, my birth control spell was still effective, if a little less so considering I had magical soulmates now, but it would hold until either a marriage took place, or I took a counter spell.

Dear Goddess, I cannot raise a child right now with Alec sulking upstairs. Please have pity on me.

"Jasmine, I am *talking to you*."

I cleared my throat and tried to focus on something other than a tiny Alec tormenting me all day. "Sorry, what were you saying?"

She erupted like a volcano, and I heard what I assumed was the entire block blowing up like a bomb before the phone changed hands.

"Beatrix, darling, I'd prefer it if we didn't have to remake the kitchen again," Aldrich soothed, his voice close to the phone's microphone. "Jasmine, love, how are you?" Dad #3 said to me, sounding pleasant despite the tirade coming from my mother that I could still hear, intermixed with Dad #2, Bosley, trying desperately to console her before her magic burned everything to a crisp. "Are you eating enough?"

"Dad, I'm at a mansion. There's staff for the staff."

He chuckled and I heard more scuffles, more Bosley consoling, until the room had quieted down. "Wolfgang told us what happened at the dance."

I rolled my eyes, because of course the Headmaster had ratted me out. "I didn't want you to worry."

Aldrich sighed. "Jasmine..." He paused, trying to piece his words together. "You know Bosley and I try not to parent you, especially since you're a grown woman now." His tone had me frozen on the rug because he never talked like this. "Darling, you just got your magic back. You're pushing yourself too much, you're being too hard on yourself. If you were newly specialized at thirteen years old, you wouldn't have the power or practice to cast a resurrection, and you can't expect that of yourself when you're newly specialized at twenty. You're young, and you're going to make mistakes. The only difference is that your power is over life and death. No other witch has that kind of responsibility with their magic, and I appreciate that you're not taking it lightly, but..." He sighed again and shifted the phone against his ear. "You have to give yourself time to improve."

I mumbled thanks for the advice and ended the call after my mom had cooled off long enough to say goodbye. Whether it was Aldrich's words, the call, or *whatever*, I was itching to move. I got up and walked the short distance to the front doors, going outside to the large stone patio. Before it lay an expansive lawn, so green it almost hurt my eyes to look at. Whoever the grounds keeper was needed to chill the eff out.

Unable to stomach looking at the artificial green, I veered off to the right, towards the forest where I hoped to find a certain wolf. What was he even doing out here? Running? Peeing on trees? Humping stuff? I protested humping that didn't involve me.

I was soon stepping inside the forest, the shift from GREEN to dull brown so drastic, it was almost eerie. The trees had a haunting glow, which seemed almost ghost-like, and I felt angry as I remembered Gilbert piddling around in the attic instead of spending time with me. Angrily stomping my feet, I continued further into the woods, looking everywhere for my giant silver wolf mate.

"Pierce?" I hissed, crouching behind a tree when I heard a noise. I peeked out and tried to see what was moving, hoping it wasn't something that would take a bite out of me. "Pierce, is that you? Growl twice if it's you." Whatever it was stayed silent, and I kept moving.

The further I went, the more a chill went up my spine. I'd never been afraid of the forest, but recent events had changed me, and the dense trees had me fearful of what was hidden behind them. Centaurs? Gorgons? Unicorns? They might look pretty, but unicorns were not friendly, not even a little.

"Jaz?"

I whirled when I heard my name called and fell head over heels until my ass was on the ground and my knee was stinging in pain. Pierce slowly appeared from around a tree trunk, and I was grateful the voice was him and not a specter, or something equally heinous.

"Pierce!" I shouted, trying to stand and wincing as my raw hand cried out from me putting weight on it.

Pierce came closer, holding his hands out to me and anxiously looking around us. "Jaz, shush! You can't come in here and draw attention to yourself! It's not safe." He reached out to help me up, flipping my hands over in his and revealing the small cuts on my palms. I cast a small spell to heal my wounds enough where they wouldn't reopen until I could get back to the mansion and find a healing potion.

"I'm sorry," I whispered, pulling him closer to me so we could hear each other. "I..." Gulping, I tried to look down at the Ouija pointer necklace I'd given him instead of staring into his brown eyes. He still made my stomach flutter, even though we'd had sex several times.

Pierce was several inches shorter than me with my boots on. He put his hands to my chin and brought my face to his, making my stomach flop around, and catching my breath in my lungs as he leaned up and gently pressed his lips to mine. I hungrily deepened our kiss, folding myself into his body and pulling him closer with my hands around his waist.

Dear god, I wanted him. I was about to let him rip my clothes off and take me on the forest floor with the risk of getting grass in my butt crack. I didn't even care. Sadly, he gave me one last kiss and rested our foreheads together, breathing my scent in with a face that made me want his lips on mine again. He roughly brought me as close as our bodies allowed, my breasts against his chest and his pelvis flush with mine. He was *definitely* also wanting that forest floor screw.

His hot breath warmed my lips, and his hand curled across my lower back. "I want you. *God*, I'm about to die if I can't have you *right now*." His other hand fisted into my long curls, almost hurting from the tugging, but it was only serving to turn me on even more. My skin felt tight as every lick of heat settled between my thighs, and Pierce's nostrils flared when he smelled my arousal.

Right when I was about to plant my hand on the front of his pants, he stepped away and my mouth dropped open. "Wha? I thought you wanted to screw?"

He appeared mournful at our loss of contact, but he didn't come back to me. "It's not safe in the forest. We're not the only creatures in here, and I can't risk your safety like that."

"Then let's go where it is safe! For Christ's sake, Pierce, *I am as wet as a damn faucet right now!*" I pointed at my neglected lady bits for emphasis. As an answer, or lack there-of, he held out his hand for me to take and led me through the forest, back towards the mansion. "What were you doing in here anyway?" I asked absently, walking behind him with our hands clasped between us as we side stepped vines and branches.

He didn't answer for a minute, perking his head up at every noise nearby that wasn't my klutzy feet trying not to trip over the forest floor. "I was, ahh..." He paused, I thought to check on another sound, but he gave me a quick look over his shoulder. "We should get back." As we reached the edge of the forest, we stopped next to the green lawn. Pierce brought me in for another warm embrace, studying my face and wiping a few curls out of my eyes. My chest warmed when he leaned up to kiss my forehead. "Not that I'm emasculated by being short, but you should start wearing flats. I keep having to raise up on my tiptoes to kiss you."

"I'll wear flats if you answer an important question for me." His eyebrows raised, his fingers massaging my back, spreading warm tingles all over me. "Why do you not get undressed before you shift? It's been bothering me, and I don't know enough about Lycans to find the answer."

He laughed and tried to stifle it with a hand over his

mouth. "Why didn't you think to ask that before? We've been together for two weeks!"

"Well, you know, I was a little busy with school, flirting, and... stuff. I didn't notice before." He smiled with another chuckle, and the gentle look he was giving me... it was typically the look someone had before they said those three words I'd warned my soulmates to not say. Still though, I felt anticipation as the moment went on, and it was almost as if I *wanted* Pierce to say it.

Crazy talk.

Before anything else could happen, the sound of a car engine interrupted us, and we peered through the edge of the woods to see a rather expensive car pull up the driveway and stop next to the patio.

I opened my mouth and turned back to Pierce, intent on getting my answer, but he was already shifted to his wolf form, and my god, he was massive.

His wolf was pretty big too. Wink.

Wolf Pierce had a cheeky look on his face, his body level with my shoulders. He definitely wouldn't have to tip toe a kiss in this form.

We left the forest behind and walked across the lawn, but by the time we reached the patio, the car was gone and whoever had just arrived was already inside the house.

It seemed the car travelers were Alec's parents, Lord and Lady Claus, or at least I assumed so because when I got back to my room, I found an invitation sitting on top of the bed.

Pierce jumped on to the sheets and started panting as I opened the envelope, but before I could start reading beyond something about attending breakfast, I was interrupted by a crash from upstairs that was definitely Alec throwing things, or rearranging his furniture, and it wasn't the first time he'd made such noises in the past week. I left Pierce in my room, stomped to the staircase, and took the polished wooden steps two at a time until I was up on the third landing where Alec's room was.

His door was open, and there was a random scattering of crumpled papers on the hallway floor, another of which sailed in front of me as I approached, and the paper smacked into the wall opposite the door before rolling and coming to a stop. Ignoring the littered floor, I stepped into Alec's room and discovered that it had much of the same carpet decorations as the hallway, only there were also books, clothes, and basically everything he owned on the floor as well.

"Did some weird shelf emptying tornado come through here?" I asked as I surveyed the area to see where Alec was. His tousled head popped up on the other side of his bed, and from his extremely messy hair, the light stubble growing on his jawline, to the dark circles under his eyes, Alec was the most unkempt I'd ever seen him in our short time together.

As my stomach fluttered at the sight of him, he stood, ran a hand through his hopeless locks, and strode over to his desk where he crumpled and threw another drawing that skittered past my feet. "What do you want, Jaz?" His smooth British accent didn't make his tone any less salty.

Though I'd come in there utterly pissed at him for abandoning me during a week-long pout, seeing him made all the anger disappear. "I heard a noise, I just wanted to see if you were okay."

An ironic laugh burst from his lips and he pushed his unbuttoned sleeves up to his elbows. Watching him expose his arms like that had me feeling like a repressed Victorian maiden, and I shook my head to maintain focus. "What makes you think I'm not okay?" he asked dryly.

I shrugged, trying not to stare at his arms. "I see you when you're sleeping. I know when you're awake."

Unlike his usual demeanor, he looked about as amused at my joke as he would an impromptu prostate exam. "If you're here to make jokes, you can just leave." He turned away and strode over to the bathroom.

"I'm sorry." The words slipped out without a thought, and Alec stopped like I'd hit him with a freezing spell, slowly moving to face me, the hollow expression he had prompting me to keep talking. "I'm sorry that I acted the way that I did, and I'm sorry I upset you. Everything you said on the train was true." My vision was starting to blur with unshed tears. "Alec, I'm the only necromancer, and if I can't do my job, if I can't fulfill my purpose, then what am I? Just an ordinary witch with ordinary powers? I may be brand new at this, but I can't help feeling like a complete failure."

Aldrich's advice had comforted me, and I knew he was right, but it didn't remove the one thing I was afraid of. It was something I couldn't tell my parents, something I could only confide to someone I trusted, to my soulmates.

"I'm terrified, Alec. I'm terrified that something will happen to someone I care about, and I won't be able to save them."

Through my blurry vision, Alec's arms came around me, his large hand covering the back of my curly head, and he slowly kissed my forehead.

"I know it seems like I'm up here pouting because of what happened, but in reality, I feel as if I failed you, and I hate the way I reacted on the train. That's not the man I want to be anymore, and you have no reason to apologize to me about it. There's also the fact that I'm getting just a tad moody, considering..." He trailed off and his spare hand moved from my shoulder down to the small of my back. Even though it made a shiver run through me as my body lit up from his touch, I pulled back to narrow my eyes at him.

"*Seriously?*"

He clicked his tongue defensively and his tangled curls fell over one of his steel eyes. "Do you know how long it's been since I had sex?"

"I think I've got you beat there," Gilbert retorted from the doorway, having returned from his new home in the attic. Wolf Pierce was by his side, who quickly came inside the room, shut the door with his snout, and shifted into a man before Alec's hand could slide down my ass cheek.

Pierce's smirk stopped that hand short. "I'm definitely excluded from that competition."

"Wha…" Alec went stiff and he whirled on me so quickly, I had to take a step back before he knocked me over. "*You had sex with Pierce already?* Where was I? Was it here? *Did you fuck in my parent's house without me?*"

"I mean," Pierce answered, drawing Alec's murderous glare to him. "It wasn't inside the *house*."

Alec ground his teeth together, holding back whatever he was about to say, so I grabbed his nose and pulled him to face me. "I'm sorry, what am I, a pinball machine? You don't have first dibs for putting your quarter in the slot, Santa Claus."

His glare deepened and he held out a warning finger

to me. "Next time you call me that, I'm putting you over my knee and spanking you until you beg me to stop."

Oh, dear goddess.

Despite the shiver running over me, I stood up on my tiptoes and leaned close to his face to match his challenge. "We'll see who punishes who, package boy." That close to him, a fragrant scent wafted over me, indicating he hadn't showered in a while. I stepped back and pinched my nose between my fingers. "You need a bath."

Alec narrowed his eyes at me. "I don't appreciate the comments. I'll bathe when I bathe."

Still holding my nose, I checked the clock on the wall. "We have to be at breakfast in an hour. Your mom sent an invitation. A fucking invitation, Alec. *For her own home*."

"That's mum for you," he snarked.

"If you take a bath, I'll take my shirt off," I offered, and he raised his eyebrows, almost looking interested.

"I'm noticing a pattern of you offering sexual favors in order to get what you want."

Smiling sweetly despite my fingers clutched around my nostrils, I raised an eyebrow at him. "You mean you *don't* want to see me in my bra?"

The dullness in his expression was smoothly replaced by his haughty sex face as he slowly perused my body, stopping at my lips, and the quick flick of his eyes up to mine had me panting. "The only place I want to see your bra is on this floor."

Sorry, bra, you're dead to me now.

I squeaked when I tried to respond, cleared my throat, and pretended it hadn't happened. "Bath first, then your reward."

Alec's mouth curved into a smile that deflated when Pierce came up behind me, wrapping his arms around my waist and nibbling on my ear. Was Alec... jealous? Gilbert was definitely still pissed about sharing me, but Alec had never seemed to care.

The warlock's face went blank and he tilted his chin up. "I'll be quick. You should go downstairs." He gave a brief look at my shoulder where Pierce's head was and left for the bathroom, slamming the door behind him.

AN INVITATION TO BREAKFAST

Alec appeared an hour later, on the dot, sliding a jacket over his freshly buttoned shirt, looking pristine as always, as if nothing had happened. His wet hair was combed and slicked to the side, those devil-may-care curls styled to perfection. He'd left the stubble, which was an interesting choice considering how clean cut he always looked. The short beard was doing him all sorts of favors, however, so I was definitely *not* complaining.

As he approached, he barely looked at me, turning his attention towards the closed dining room door as he straightened his sleeves. Pierce was at my feet in his wolf form and could offer no comfort beyond rubbing against my hand.

I opened my mouth to say something about how good the warlock looked when the doors in front of us opened, revealing a long dining table full to the brim with breakfast treats. Alec's parents were already there, sitting on one side of the table. Lady Claus looked as pristine as her son, with not a single grey hair out of place, and she looked dressed for an evening out instead of a casual breakfast at home. Her husband, Lord Claus, had on a suit that was similar to Alec's, completing the Claus triangle of perfection.

And then there was me, the girl who usually ate breakfast while wearing an oversized taco cat shirt that shows way too much side boob, and bunny slippers. Knowing the Claus penchant for being well dressed, I'd opted for one of my many black dresses, one with a pentagram design across the chest, but I still felt underdressed. Lady Claus amplified that when she gave me a once over as Alec and I came to the other side of the table, her thin eyebrow lifting slightly, enough to make it clear she thought I was dressed improperly.

Sorry, I must've left my breakfast ballgown at home.

"Mother, father," Alec greeted with a nod of his head. I chose a seat across from Lady Claus, and Alec helped me push it in before he sat next to me. "I trust your trip went well?"

Lady Claus's pinched look softened as she focused on

her son and pretended I wasn't there. "It was quite satisfactory."

Dear god, were we really going to sit here and make *small talk?* Ugh, small talk was the worst. Maybe if I stabbed my hand with my fork, we could skip it altogether.

"I trust you two will be returning to school tomorrow?" Lord Claus said casually, his words laced with a tone that didn't match the placid look on his face. "Wolfgang assured us you would be able to make up the lessons you've missed, but if you miss too many, it might affect your marks."

"And we wouldn't want that, now would we?" Alec muttered under his breath, but if either of his parents heard it, they didn't react. Surely, they knew why we'd left school after what happened at the dance.

I studied Lady Claus, the way she delicately speared some eggs and brought them to her mouth while keeping her eyes on the tablecloth, and Alec's hand came over mine, rubbing his thumb along my skin.

"Jaz needed some time away from school, and I was more than happy to give it to her, whether or not it affected my studies," Alec explained smoothly, the warmth of his hand spreading through me.

Lord Claus continued as if his son hadn't spoken, turning his stare to me. "Now that you two are betrothed, I trust you'll be moving into our estate, Jasmine? Seeing as how you're not an heiress, and you'll be taking the Claus name once the marriage has taken place, that is."

I bristled and couldn't help but wonder if that's what Alec expected as well. I had no intention of taking anyone's name. I would remain a Neck until the day I died. Plus, Alec hadn't even proposed. None of them had. We hadn't even said the L word yet, so first things first, Daddy Santa.

"Actually," Alec began, drawing both of his parents' attention, and they weren't pleased at him continuing the conversation, if their sour looks were anything to go by. "I shall be taking Jaz's name, as is expected of a proper soulmate."

Lady Claus delicately flinched and attempted a smile to hide her repulsion. "She's not an heiress, Alec."

"Not to mention, taking her name means turning our estate over to her. It would become the Neck estate," Lord Claus stated with irritation, the top of his head turning bright red. "Surely you cannot suggest erasing hundreds of years of our family's history."

Alec's hand squeezed mine before he moved it away, straightening his jacket to mask himself. "It is symbolic of my commitment to her. I am no longer my own, I am hers. If you have a problem with that, I suggest you find another heir. Oh wait, there are none."

Looking down at my bowl of oatmeal, I could feel both of them glaring at me as if the entire conversation had been my idea, but all I could think about was Alec standing up to his parents and showing everyone his bond to me. My father had done the same, taking my mother's name and leaving his family estate behind, all because of the love he felt for his soulmate.

And Alec had done that for me.

He and his parents continued eating, but I could only admire Alec's perfectly adorable face, smiling like an idiot at him as my heart warmed in a way I'd tried to ignore before. Alec didn't notice me staring at him until he was finished eating, and his frown melted instantly when he saw the look of desire growing on my face.

Take me upstairs right now and show me what you're made of.

As if he could hear my thoughts, his sexy face was back, and his expression was far too heated for mixed company, especially considering that mixed company was his *parents*. He looked at me like he was going to devour me whole, and it ignited me right to my core.

Without breaking eye contact with me, Alec lifted the carefully placed napkin from across his knees and smoothly tossed it onto his plate. "Excuse us, Jaz and I should probably pack our things." He quickly stood as I did the same and we almost collided in our haste to leave the room. Alec's hands came around my waist once we'd made it to the hallway and he flipped me over in his arms as he lifted one hand behind us to shut the dining room doors. "This is a fine way to end breakfast, though I'm not sure what brought this on. Not that I'm complaining."

"Just shut up and *fucking kiss me*!" Grabbing handfuls of his tousled curls, I roughly pulled his lips to mine, crashing our teeth together, our kiss so desperate, so frantic, it was like we'd been apart for years instead of a week. I just needed him all over me, inside me, on top of me.

My feet lifted off the ground and my stomach left my body as Alec took flight with me in his arms, making me tighten my grip on him. We zipped up two flights of stairs before making it to Alec's room. The door magically slammed shut behind us, and then the silkiness of sheets was underneath me as he placed me on top of his bed.

All thought left my head, there was only my desperate need for Alec, something primal and deep, the likes of which I'd never felt before. Not with Pierce. Not with Gilbert. Not anyone. It was like a firecracker, white hot and bursting.

With a few grunts of frustration, I heard Alec's belt clink, felt his hands on my hips as he removed my panties, and then he was gone. I opened my eyes to see him staring down at me, his chest heaving with excitement, drawing my attention to the bulge straining against his boxers. I noted that it appeared tasty enough to eat, and looked back up at him through the curtain of my lashes, his heated gaze still on me.

"You," he began in a husky tone that made me tremble with excitement. "Jasmine Neck, you are the most beautiful person I've ever seen. I never thought for one moment that someone like you would be my *magicae equidem*, because I didn't think I deserved perfection. And now I get to spend the rest of my life serving you."

I exhaled deeply, sliding my tongue along my teeth, and flipped back some of my pink tipped curls. "Cut the chit chat and *fuck me*."

With our eyes locked, he reached down to his boxers and pulled his cock out, watching me look down at it and back up at him. Given his usual demeanor, I expected some teasing, his practiced smirk, making me suffer by waiting until I begged. Alec did none of those things.

He came closer and leaned over me, hovering just above my lips as he pulled me forward with two hands, roughly gripping my hips until I was right on the edge of the bed. My legs trembled when he settled between them, and just as I felt his fingertips moving from my inner thighs to right where I was dripping with need, my magic started escaping from me, as it had when we first kissed.

Small amounts of my power waved and dipped when he brushed over my swollen nub, only adding to the sensations Alec was giving me. His fingertips were replaced by the velvet hardness of his cock, and he slowly rubbed the tip up and down my slit, my magic responding in such a way that I felt short of breath, almost like it was as much of a thirsty bitch for Alec as I was. That became even more apparent when Alec sucked my bottom lip into his mouth and slid his hard cock inside my wet sheath, making my magic explode like a shaken soda.

If magical orgasms were a thing, I was having one.

I threw my head back and erupted in groans as Alec struggled to keep me steady, and I saw his power come out to contain mine, his tendrils soothing my magic enough to let me catch my breath.

"Jesus, I can barely keep both our magics contained," Alec breathed, resting our foreheads together, and beads of Alec's sweat fell onto my skin.

I tilted my head up to look into his steel eyes. "Then don't. Let it all out."

Alec's expression dissolved into pure lust, smoke puffed out of his nostrils like a dragon, and he withdrew only to slam himself back into me. He let my magic go as he started fucking me, unable to focus on it with me mewling beneath him.

He kissed a path down my neck and my eyes fluttered open to watch his magic floating and dancing against mine like the flames of a fire. I felt everything our magic did as clearly as I felt Alec's lips sucking my skin, and it made every sensation so intense, he had barely begun a breathless rhythm before I was ready to explode.

He groaned when I squealed as the pressure built inside me. It enveloped me until everything else fell away. I only existed for this moment with Alec, this moment that was going to shatter me from the inside out. One of my hands fisted into the red silken sheets, holding on for dear life as I felt myself starting to crest, the other hand coming around Alec's neck to steady me.

Caught in that moment before climax, unable to go back and craning to go forward, each thrust inside me brought an explosion from my magic, and Alec's power answered with an equally intense burst.

"By the goddess, more, Alec, *more*," I moaned, my throat starting to feel sore from the sounds I was making. Alec turned my head with his hand on my throat and hungrily devoured my lips, the movement of his body jostling our mouths together. Every few seconds he broke off in a heady moan, rising in volume and intensity just as I was.

I inhaled sharply, feeling myself finally there, arching my back and tossing my head back, pulling on the sheets, and with a few more thrusts from Alec's insanely skillful cock, a blinding orgasm washed over me, causing my magic to erupt in a sonic boom. Alec's soon followed with his own climax, and he raggedly gave a few more strokes inside me as he came, his throat hoarse by the time he rested his sweaty head against my shoulder.

Both struggling to catch our breath as hot desire ran over our bodies, Alec smoothly gripped my waist and dragged us into the center of the bed to delicately collapse atop one another. His leg was across one of mine, my hand was flopped on top of his face. He made a spitting noise and I twisted my head to the side, watching him pull strands of my curls from his mouth.

"Christ, witch," he breathed, running his hands through his damp locks. "I've never had sex like that before. One thrust in and I was ready to come, but magically, and I say that with complete irony, I couldn't until you did. God, it was exquisite torture. If that's what sex with you is going to be like, we're never leaving this bed."

"Not even to pee?"

"Wow," someone said. "That was a great thing to walk into." We both shot up from the bed to see human Pierce by the door, and a semi-transparent Gilbert right beside him, giving me a look that made a shiver run across my heated skin.

"Actually, we came in before you finished fucking,"

Gilbert noted smugly in his British accent. "You couldn't hear the door over Alec's moaning."

Pierce's dark eyes dipped to where my dress skirt was still pulled up, just barely showing my small amount of pubic hair. I almost covered myself up, but since all three had seen my snatch before then, I just leaned back on my hands and hoped they got a nice view.

"It's all part of my plan to seduce you, Pierce," Alec said smoothly, eyeing the Lycan like he was a juicy steak. A steak he wanted to make out with and fuck.

Gilbert crossed his ghostly arms over his chest. "Not even going to try it on me? Rude."

"I appreciate the effort, even though it's wasted." Pierce just slightly looked towards Alec's lap where his softened dick lay outside his pants, and Alec more than noticed the switch of Pierce's gaze from my vagina to warlock penis.

That smirk of his curled up Alec's face. "Wanna compare sizes while you're busy staring at my wick?"

Pierce quickly looked up at the ceiling. "I'm about as big as my wolf, comparatively, not that this is a competition."

"Extra-large, very nice," Alec purred. "I'm more of a large myself."

"I've got a medium dick," Gilbert piped in, making me quirk an eyebrow at him because *that* wasn't true. "It can talk to ghosts." I choked on my saliva and erupted in a laughing fit, falling onto the bed and probably giving the boys a nice view of my bare ass.

"If I could fist bump you, that just earned one," Alec mused beside me. Once I'd stopped laughing, I rolled to face him and he ran his fingers through my hair. We shared a brief smile before Pierce came up behind me, tugging me into his arms and giving me a playful bite on the shoulder. Alec watched with amused interest, a hint of desire rising in his eyes. "We need to pack, we're going back to Highborn tonight. Unless," he added, checking my face. "You'd rather not? We can stay longer if you need more time."

I hesitated just long enough that all three of them moved in reaction. Pierce lifted me to sit on the bed, still holding me from behind. Alec scooted closer to me, taking my hand, and Gilbert floated over to sit beside him, just barely taking my other hand, hovering above the red sheets.

With them around me like that, I was covered from all sides. I felt safe, protected, emotions I had rarely felt before. They all waited for me to speak what I was feeling, ready for whatever answer I gave them, and ready to pick me up if I fell apart again. My mouth opened and closed several times as I tried to think of what to say. Opening up wasn't easy for me, and it was something I'd have to get used to.

"I don't know if I'm okay yet, but…" I swallowed,

and somehow Gilbert's hand gained strength on mine until he felt as real as Alec did, minus the warmth. "We should still go back. No matter what happens, I'll be fine as long as you three are with me."

And that's what I kept telling myself as we packed to leave.

※

LESS THAN AN HOUR LATER, ALEC STOOD BESIDE ME AT the closest train station with wolf Pierce against my leg and the ghostly Gilbert hovering behind us. Lord and Lady Claus had given us a dull send-off, mostly emphasizing that Alec needed to keep his grades up and asking when we were getting married. Lady Claus still had no warmth for me, probably because having a necromancer for a daughter-in-law was ruining her social standing amongst the magical Karens.

Just wait until she found out about Pierce.

"I'm working on something," Alec said suddenly, startling me by breaking his pensive silence after so long. "If I can do it, I think you'll be pleased. It'll mean time in the library, which as you know, I'd rather be kicked off the astronomy tower before I do that."

"Are you trying to impress me by reading books?"

He gasped at me, his mouth popping open and his eyes widening in shock. "As if I'd even *need* to do that to impress you, and even if I did, I still wouldn't do it. You take that back." I patronized him with a pat on his blue jacket sleeve, and he narrowed his eyes at me as I continued patting him. "I will ask that all three of you keep this a secret."

"Diva," I whispered with an eye roll. "May I ask what is so important that you have to read something, *le gasp*."

His eyes darted to my skirt where Pierce was nomming on the edge of it, and back up at the green field in front of us. "I'd rather not say, in case I can't do it. I don't want to get your hopes up."

Smiling slightly, I heard the distant sound of the train whistle. "Look at you, being all considerate. I kinda like it."

Alec smirked at me and picked up one of my bags when the train's whistle got closer. "I thought you liked me better as an asshole," he commented sweetly.

I leaned near the edge of the platform to see if I could spot the train, and saw it curving around a turn, almost at the station. "It depends on if you have your hand down my pants."

With an ear-splitting whistle, the Incantation Express rolled in, bringing with it a whoosh of air that sent me back a few steps, and Pierce was right behind me to keep me from falling over. Alec wasted no time boarding the train with the wispy Gilbert trailing behind him, but my feet refused to move as I remembered where we were going.

We were going back to school. Back to the dining hall. Back to where the centaur's body had been. Was the room still destroyed, or had they fixed everything in the week we'd been gone? At least I knew the body wasn't there anymore, but that wouldn't erase the memory of it.

Pierce whined under my hand, nosing my side with his snout and letting out a bark that made Alec and Gilbert turn from inside the train entrance.

Alec set my bags down and stepped back onto the platform, holding his hand out to me. "Jaz." I gripped Pierce's fur and slowly lifted my eyes to Alec's steel gaze. "We're right here with you."

Inhaling deeply to gather my strength, I put one foot in front of the other until I could take Alec's warm hand. After retrieving our bags, he guided me onto the train and to an empty compartment that he locked once we were all inside. He drew the curtain on the small window to give us privacy, and Pierce was turned into a human and hugging me tightly before I could sit down.

The Lycan leaned back, pushing some of my pink tipped curls over my shoulder, and giving a quick look at my feet to note with a smile that I was wearing flats as he'd asked. He didn't have to reach up to kiss my forehead. "In answer to your question from before, I don't need to get undressed to shift, it's a perk of being a Lycan. That night we met, Alec made a note to tell me he was glad about it because then you wouldn't see my dick."

Alec let out a quick gasp before walking to sit on one of the seats. "Not sure where that comment came from, but *nark much?*"

"Things are heating up on this week's episode of *'who gets more jealous at having to share Jaz,'*" I snarked as I waved my pointer finger around.

Someone knocked on the compartment door and I screamed in surprise before shoving Pierce against the wall next to the door. Alec had a look of amusement as he answered it.

"Any sweets today?" the candy lady asked, assuming incorrectly that anyone would want butt flavored candy. Alec must've humored her because he had three lollipops in his hand when he straightened and re-locked the door.

I leaned one hand against Pierce's chest and narrowed my eyes at the offending treats Alec held. "You know those taste like ass, right? Like, I know you've only recently started riding the train, but the candy here is shit."

Alec maintained eye contact with me as he pulled the plastic wrapper off one of the candies and gave it a slow lick exactly the way I wanted him to lick me.

"Funny of you to assume I've never eaten ass." He contemplated the taste of the lollipop and took another lick. "Must've changed the recipe, all I taste is pussy."

Pierce held out a hand and Alec tossed him the second candy. "Well," he said after sticking it in his mouth. "Alec is right. Definitely snatch flavored. Yours tastes better though."

They continued sucking on the treats with Gilbert and me gaping at them, only to be interrupted by Pierce's cellphone ringing. He pushed the lollipop into his cheek and pulled the phone from his pocket to check the screen.

"Gotta take this," he announced around the candy in his mouth. "Alec, is it safe for me to run to the bathroom?"

"I'll take you." The warlock handed me the last lollipop and they left together, closing the door behind them. I twirled the candy around in my hands, unwilling to test the flavor, even if it was apparently a better recipe. When I sat down on one of the seats, Gilbert floated to sit next to me, and I was able to lean my head against his transparent shoulder.

Smiling at the questionable candy, I continued playing with it. "Seems like the more I'm able to touch you, the easier it becomes," I noted as his grey fingers came across me, and he took the candy, only to toss it over his shoulder where it landed on the compartment floor.

Before I could stand to retrieve it, Gilbert's fingers forcefully turned my chin to face him. "The more you touch me, the more I want you. I want to know what you taste like. I want to know what you feel like when I thrust myself deep inside you. The longer I have to wait to know those things, the more insane I feel. Insane for you." I squeaked as my brain turned to mush under the intensity of his gaze.

"Dear god, please stay like this forever," I whispered, completely hypnotized. His fingers on my chin pulled me to him where he kissed me long and slow, his other hand tangling into my curls, using them to keep me still. "I missed you so much, you were so mean staying in the attic and not letting me see you."

He hummed against my lips and held me there, hovering above my face as he studied me. "I know, I feel awful about it. But I just need the solitude sometimes, I'm not sure what it is, but every time I come back, I feel more... more like myself. It's been that way since I first, how do you put it, woke up as a ghost?"

"More like yourself, meaning less whiny?" I teased slightly, breaking free from his grip on me just enough where I was able to kiss his cold lips, their frost turning into flames that licked over my skin.

"Yes to that, but can you blame me when I've been wanting you for so long and someone else got you first? That's enough to make anyone a whiny bitch." I closed my eyes to steal another kiss from him, and suddenly the hand on my hair was gone, sending me crashing face first into the seat cushion. "Sorry," Gilbert said from above my head. He was hovering above me when I rolled over and opened my eyes, giving me an apologetic smile even though I knew he was as frustrated as I was. "Ran out of juice."

Shutting my eyes, I whined and slumped my arms down onto the bench. "I wanted more cuddles." The ghost lowered himself until a chill settled over my entire body, and a delicate icy feeling ran over my lips. Was he licking them?

"You'll have to suffice with me, then," Alec pronounced as he came back into the compartment, only to find Gilbert on top of my body but unable to touch me. "Performance issues?" Gilbert straightened to hover nearby and glared at the warlock, watching Alec come to sit next to me. He set my head in his lap and started stroking my long curls in thought.

"Where's Pierce?" I asked, trying to sit up but Alec put a hand on my shoulders to stop me.

"He's on a phone call. Wouldn't say who it was, but it must be important for him to risk being seen. He promised he'd shift back when he leaves the lavatory so no one will notice him, but there's hardly anyone around. No one rides the train if they can help it."

"Yes, thank you for reminding me that I'm a basic bitch who doesn't own a magical car." I flicked his nose with my pointer finger and he captured my hand, slowly kissing each finger and every spot on my palm.

"I have three cars, and they'll all be yours when you take over my estate. You'll never want for anything ever again. No more pussy candy train."

I giggled and took my hand back to run my fingertips over his stubble. A smile curved up my lips as he looked down at me with his playboy steel eyes. "You didn't have to do that for me," I told him. I loved that he was willing to turn over his estate to me, but I still felt like it was unnecessary. "You don't have to take my name, or make me the Claus heir. It certainly put a bee up your parent's pants."

"Yes, and then you tore *my* pants off afterwards. Like I'm going to give up sex like that by not going through with it." He kissed my hand again and laid it across my stomach, stroking my hair and relaxing me with every touch of his fingers. "This is what I want. You're the center of my world now. If I kept my name or my estate, that would dishonor our bond. I'd be a worthless soulmate if I didn't do this."

"I couldn't have said it better myself," Gilbert chimed in, drawing our gazes to him. "I've remembered a bit more about the magical world during my time in the attic. Alec is correct. We take your name, and all of our worldly goods belong to you. Anything less would be insulting. Maybe things were different when I was alive, whenever that was, but I still feel strongly about it. I'll be Gilbert Neck from now on."

"Sappy," I admonished with a soft smile. "And you can't take my name unless we're married." Alec opened his mouth to say something and was interrupted by a loud noise in the hallway.

A muffled voice came through our door. "Sir, there are others that need to use the lavatory, please return to your compartment."

Alec and I almost collided with each other as we got up from the seat, clamoring to get to the door. He got to it first, and we ran out to the hallway where several witches were gathered outside the bathroom doors.

The ticket master rapped his fist against the men's room door again. "Sir, if you do not exit the lavatory, I will use a spell to open this door."

"Ladies and gentlemen!" Alec shouted, drawing their attention over to him, and he nudged me with his hand to motion me towards the bathrooms. "I am an Illusionist, a rare specialty. You are all in for a treat." He slapped his hands together and a flurry of butterflies came out of them, flying amongst the small crowd. With everyone enthralled over the butterflies, I took that small moment to reach the men's room.

"Pierce," I whispered against the wood, checking over my shoulder to make sure no one was looking at me. The door opened slightly, and Pierce's tanned hand shot out to take mine, squeezing my fingers for reassurance. He tugged me into the bathroom, staying behind the door so no one would see him, and he pulled me in a hug once the door was closed.

His arms trembled against my back while something wet touched my forehead, tears that were rolling down his cheeks. "I thought they would find me. I thought I'd never see you again." He started talking in Korean to soothe both of us, and though I didn't understand the words, I still felt comforted. "Oppa is sorry he almost got caught."

"Oppa?" I looked up at him and wiped at his wet face.

"Boyfriend," he translated with a sheepish grin.

Smiling, I leaned our foreheads together and kissed his lips, enjoying that they were right there for me and I didn't have to reach up for them like I did with Alec. "You should shift back," I said between kisses. As much as I usually wanted him to shove me against the wall and have his way with me, we'd already flirted danger once that day. We didn't need a second time.

"I tried, I'm too shaken. I have to calm down first."

He let me go and took a step back towards the sink. Alec chose that moment to open the door and swiftly slide in before locking it behind him. He strode over to Pierce and pulled the Lycan to him for a hug, one that Pierce quickly reciprocated.

Had Alec seduced him when I wasn't looking?

Before I could get mad at either of them, Alec glanced down at me and grinned that playboy smirk of his. "Purely platonic, my love. I can give him the illusion of calm, but he has to be in my arms." They continued hugging, every second making Pierce more relaxed until he slumped against Alec's suit. "That's a good boy, Pierce." Alec raised a hand to Pierce's long brown hair and stopped himself before he ran his fingers through it, as he did with my curls. He clearly still wanted some wolf in his diet. "Gilbert and I won't let you be found out. We'll do whatever is necessary to keep you safe. As much as it pains me to say this... the three of us are brothers now, Lycan or no. You're our family."

Pierce stepped away and wiped at his cheeks. "Thank you, Alec." The warlock nodded to him. "I'm still not interested."

"Damn," Alec said under his breath, and we watched Pierce shift into a wolf. With him safe, Alec led us to the door and held out his arm to keep me behind him before cracking it open and stepping out.

"Behold!" he shouted, and smoke burst from his

nostrils like a dragon, crowding the hallway with it. With the smoke filling my eyesight, Alec grabbed my hand, pulling me along through the mist with Pierce by my side, and we escaped into our compartment, safe. For now.

THE SOULMATE DORM

The Incantation Express left us at the train station platform and zipped off into the countryside with a blast of its horn. All four of us still felt a bit shaken by almost being found out, and Alec wordlessly picked up our bags, walking alongside me through the station. Outside it was a waiting horse and buggy taxi he'd ordered, and he put our bags into the trunk before hopping in beside me as Gilbert and Pierce sat across from us.

"You must be the necromancer I've been hearing about," the taxi driver said from the elevated driver's seat. He shook the reins and the horse took off in a trot.

Was it my pink hair that had tipped him off? The Claus heir by my side? My giant wolf familiar?

"Never seen a ghost before, but I reckon he'd be following our new necromancer around."

Ahh, Gilbert.

"Guilty!" I shouted out so he could hear me, and he chuckled as we rolled through town.

Highborn Village was bustling with life, as it always was. The local residents were eating, talking, playing music, and enjoying their down time while everyone at the academy was still in school. Once classes were done for the day, we all migrated to the village to shop, eat, and get drunk. Mostly get drunk, in my case.

I could've used a drink right about then, because the foreboding castle that was my school came into view. Alec reached for my hand before I could work out what emotion I was feeling, but it didn't matter because the buggy stopped just outside the village. We could either stay there, or we could walk up the long path and go inside Highborn. I wanted to bolt in the other direction until I was so deep inside the woods, not even Pierce would be able to find me.

Goddess, I know I ask you for a lot of useless stuff, but a little courage would be great.

Though she gave no answer, I pretended that she had, and with squared shoulders, I jumped down from the carriage to the ground and helped Alec gather our bags. We watched the horse trot off with the driver waving to us, removing any escape plan. Sliding the straps to my coffin backpack onto my shoulders, I reached out for Alec's hand, tunneling my other in Pierce's thick fur, and I led my three men through the magical doorway.

"Hmm," Alec said in thought after we were all through. "My spell to let Pierce and Gilbert in seems to still be here, that's good. I thought what the centaurs did would've destroyed my handiwork." He turned and stared at the invisible school barrier for a few moments, studying the magic of it in a way I couldn't see. "Weird," he said under his breath, and he turned back to me, chewing his lip in thought. He walked past me up the hill, leaving me to follow behind.

Gilbert hovered over us and gave me a quick chilly kiss on the cheek. "I'll catch up with you guys later."

"So," I said, watching Gilbert float away, and I started trudging towards the school, leaning on Pierce with every step as my legs were already starting to cramp. "What's Christmas like at the Claus mansion? Do you leave a plate of cookies out for yourself?"

"Ha," was Alec's answer. We reached the entrance courtyard and he stopped to look down at me, the corner of his mouth curving into a smirk. "If I'm Santa, then you're my plate of cookies, and I'm going to eat you until it's Christmas morning."

Before I could respond, or plant my body against

him, Professor Wisniewski floated over to us with her billowing purple skirts.

"Ahh!" she exclaimed, drawing my attention away from Alec's smirk. "You two are back. The Headmaster would like to see you, he told me to send you up when you arrived." She looked down at wolf Pierce and held her hand out for him to sniff. He licked her fingers, his long tongue bigger than her forearm. "You can leave your bags in the entry hall, I'll send someone to take them to your rooms." After wiping her hand on her dress, she paused slightly, trying to be discreet about looking in my direction, as if I was a loose cannon. Okay, fine, I definitely was. "I hope you both had a lovely holiday and got plenty of rest."

I knew her inquiry would be the first of many as all the people at school who cared, or who had to *pretend* to care, would be asking how I was.

"We did, it was very relaxing," Alec answered for me, and Wisniewski left us in the courtyard, satisfied with the answer for now. "Soulmate." I looked up from the fountain to see Alec holding his hand out for me. I stepped into his arms and pressed myself against his linen suit, the smell of his aftershave making my head spin. He set the bags down, holding me with both arms, and I felt Pierce's cold nose on my leg.

"Remember I said that I don't know if I'm okay?" I began, swallowing down the thick feeling settling in my throat. "Jury is still out." Pierce whined and started shoving me towards the entrance doors. "What the hell, Pierce?" The doors opened for us, no doubt from Alec sending a spell out, and Pierce didn't stop pushing me until I was standing in the entryway, looking straight into the massive dining hall, the very place I'd been dreading to see.

It was perfect.

All of the walls were back. The chandeliers, tables, and chairs were perfectly set up. Everything looked exactly as it had before, as if nothing had happened. And it felt impossibly wrong.

Alec whistled low when he came into the entryway, setting our bags down on the stone flooring. "Seems they wasted no time fixing it."

"We couldn't very well have a wrecked dining hall." Professor Halace had made her entrance, pressing her hands to the sides of her green velvet dress, the shape of which made her appear even more drop dead gorgeous. Despite her killer dress, her face still looked as she always did, like she'd just licked a salty lemon.

She softened when she turned to me, and she quickly covered it up by raising her chin. "You two missed a week's worth of homework. If you want to pass exams, I suggest you make up the work. I've put together a packet for both of you, it's in your rooms."

I was taken aback by her consideration for us. No

doubt she did it just to torture us with schoolwork, but still, I never expected her to do anything for us, especially since she didn't like me.

"Thank you, Professor," I told her quietly. "That was very kind of you."

She blinked several times, also not expecting kindness, and the moment passed with another haughty chin raise. "Yes. Well. Be sure to get it finished. You're already behind on the school year, Jasmine."

I smiled and nodded to her. "Yep, on it. Lots of homework. If I need help, I'll come bother you."

She scowled, her mouth puckering in annoyance. "I'd rather you didn't. The Headmaster already volunteered to be your mentor, even after that dreadful incident with the crystal ball. And speaking of which, you're to report to the Headmaster immediately. Isabelle and I will see to your bags." She pointed a perfectly manicured finger over her shoulder that booked no refusals. "Off you go. *Now*."

We walked to the staircase and I strained my neck looking up to see how far we had to go. "I never thought I'd say this, Alec, but can you fly us up to the Headmaster's office? If I keep walking up and down these stairs every day, my legs will end up looking like the Rock's forearms."

My warlock lover picked me up like a newlywed bride, and we shot off the staircase like a rocket, flying up, up, up, past each floor. Pierce bounded up the steps in his wolf form, practically able to take each flight of stairs in one leap, and he reached the right landing only a few seconds before we did.

"Show off," Alec mouthed, smoothly setting me down next to him. Pierce let out a wheezing laugh, and he ignored Alec's disgruntled stare as we walked the rest of the way to the Headmaster's office.

I rapped my hand on the door and it opened automatically for me. Inside, it was still as dusty as a thirty-year-old dry spell, and as dark as a cave. My foot left a shoe print in the layer of dust on the floor.

Gag.

"Ahh, there you both are," the Headmaster exclaimed from somewhere in the room, every word lilting with his British accent. I craned to see where he was at, checking around the numerous piles of books. The walls were literally covered in massive bookshelves, so it wasn't like he didn't have room for them. Was he allergic to putting his books back? "Drinks?"

"Yep," I shouted to wherever he was at. Pierce sat beside me, sneezing from the dust.

"Apologies for the atmosphere, I rarely clean the place. If anything in here is moved, I can't find what I need."

Alec made a small blue light in his hand that he held up so he could look around the room, grimacing at the cobwebs near our heads. "And the reason why it's as dark as an ass crack in here?"

The Headmaster let out a laugh and his short body appeared from behind a pile of books, carrying a tray with three glasses and a bowl of water in his small hands. "I just prefer it." He set the tray down on a nearby stool and handed us two of the glasses, then placed the bowl in front of Pierce. My glass had red wine, and I gulped half of it in one breath. When I surfaced for air, the Headmaster was staring up at me, trying to keep his features blank, but he still had the same expression as Wisniewski, cautious and concerned. "I'm glad you two are back. Granted, I figured you would need more time after what happened, but I won't question further if you say everything is fine."

Looking down at him, I wiped my mouth against my arm and had to cough when a cloud of dust entered my throat. I washed it down with more wine. "It is." I ignored the way he studied me, trying to sniff out my bullshit, no doubt, and set my empty glass down on a nearby low table.

"You two have been assigned to a new dormitory, by the way. Soulmates don't live with the other students."

Alec snorted. "Because sex, yes?"

The Headmaster gave him a long look of annoyance. "We don't expect chastity here, as you're well aware of,

Mr. Claus. Especially when soulmates are involved. We provide an extra layer of privacy for them, as a courtesy."

"Banger," Alec responded. "Emphasis on bang."

Groaning, I rolled my eyes and wished there was more wine. "Oh my god, I'm soulmates with you."

Alec gave me a cheeky grin, swirling the wine around in his glass, one he hadn't taken a single sip of yet. "Lucky you."

"That's all we needed to discuss," the Headmaster interrupted. "You can spend the rest of the day getting moved into your new rooms, as long as you're down at the dining hall for dinner. Now scoot, I have things to do." He waved his arms at us and walked to a stool by the table that he sat down on, his short legs just barely touching the floor.

Alec led the way out and closed the door behind us, leaning against it as he crossed his arms over his chest, observing me with a slight smirk. "It seems we'll be living together now. I look forward to all those special side boob moments we're going to have."

"Rule number one of living with Jaz." I held up one finger for him and Pierce. "You drink my coffee, you die. Rule number two. We're not sharing a blanket. Ever. Rule number three."

Alec's eyebrows knit together as he stared at my fingers. "How many rules are there? I won't be able to remember them all."

"Rule number three," I reiterated, shaking my three fingers. "No sex until after coffee."

"Splendid." Alec pushed off the door and walked down the hall, back towards the stairwell. "The soulmate dorm is across the back courtyard. When the Headmaster says it's for privacy, what he really means is it's far enough away so no one will hear the screams of pleasure."

Rolling my eyes, I trudged after him with Pierce at my heels. I didn't relish the thought of a longer distance to my classes in the morning. Being late just got me in trouble. "I'm surprised you know where the soulmate dorm is."

Alec grunted and shrugged his wide shoulders, floating down the stairs without touching them. "Just because I haven't romanced any of them doesn't mean I don't know where it is. Everyone knows. There's not a student here who hasn't daydreamed about living there. Or rather, having a soulmate so you *can* live there."

"Speaking of students," I chimed once we'd gotten to the bottom of the staircase. "I don't remember you being here when I was younger. I'm certain I would've remembered that attitude of yours, coupled with the vape pen."

The warlock stuffed his hands into the pockets of his expensive suit pants. "I went to a different school before sophomore year, but I was expelled for making out behind the astronomy tower. Highborn is a bit more tolerant of such things, thus why I came here."

Color me surprised.

"Hey Alec!" a voice called out, and I noticed a group of girls standing down the hall, one of which was staring with heart eyes at the man standing next to me.

Alec didn't even blink, he continued gazing at me like he hadn't heard her. "Let's hope Halace didn't send our bags to the trash. That would be just like her."

He held out his hand for me, and with a grin, I came close to him, studying that smirky face of his. I reached up on my tiptoes to kiss his lips, full in the knowledge that he belonged to me now, and I didn't mind the idea that the most popular, most sought after boy in school was mine.

Even with his dumb sense of humor.

"Hmm," Alec buzzed against my lips. "Jealous of my fans?"

"Just enjoying that I get to kiss the sexiest boy at school." Pierce intentionally bumped against my legs, making me collide with Alec, and I whipped my head around to see the wolf hissing out a laugh at me. "*No doggie treats for you.*"

Hand in hand, Alec and I stood in front of the soulmate dorm. It looked less like a dorm and more like an apartment building, except for the single entrance door in the middle of the bottom floor.

We entered into a small lobby with mail portals on the left side, one of which was glowing bright blue. I stepped closer to it and saw it was for room 2B, with mine and Alec's name printed next to the number. Of the dozen or so room numbers on the wall, only four had names assigned to them.

Alec reached his hand into the bright mail portal and pulled out an envelope with our names on it. He opened it to find three magical keys inside, along with a note from the Headmaster.

Your new rooms will only unlock with these specific keys. There's a spare in case you lose one.

Alec passed me one of the keys and put the others in his pocket, and we went up the stairs to the second floor. The doors were very spaced out, with only four in total, much less than the advanced studies dorms had. 2B was the first on the right, and I put my key in the slot, hearing it unlock as the spell on the door was temporarily removed, then I stepped inside our new dorm.

As soon as I was inside, I knew why there were so few rooms on the floor, because it was more of an apartment than a dorm. It had a living room, a small kitchen area, a hallway with a bathroom on the right and a bedroom at the end.

Alec and Pierce came in behind me, shutting the door as I explored towards the bedroom.

"Whoa!" I heard Pierce say, having shifted back once we were safe and alone. "They do not skimp on the soulmate digs." The bedroom was spacious, the bed even more so. It looked big enough to hold five people, much bigger than two needed. Weird.

"Well, that looks cozy," Gilbert said, suddenly appearing beside me, and I sprang back, slamming my shoulder into the wall.

"Fucking Satan in a hammock, don't *do that*!" I admonished as I rubbed my shoulder. Alec had just joined us, giving the bed a heated look that he started directing at me, when someone knocked on the door. Pierce ran to shut himself into the bathroom and I went to answer the knock with Alec right behind me.

Standing in the hallway was three girls. The middle one was shorter than the other two by half a foot, and she looked so mousy and adorable, I knew Alec would've pounced on her were he not attached to me.

The next girl had an arm draped on the middle one, her fingers closed around the girl's gingham dress. She had a large tattoo on her arm, and short hair slicked over to expose the shaved side of her head.

The third girl was standing a bit away from the other two, and she was smiling at me as she ran a hand through her curls, her dark skin only a tad lighter than her hair.

"Hello!" middle girl greeted, tipping herself up on her heels. "I'm Pollyanna. This is my friend Albany," she said, gesturing to the third girl, and then turned her hand to the second girl. "And this is my soulmate, Andi."

Andi took Pollyanna's hand and gave it a kiss before she shot daggers at the boy behind me. "Santa Claus better keep his hands to himself." The snide way she said '*Santa Claus*' made me want to never say it again.

"*Andi*," Pollyanna admonished, her cheeks turning bright pink. "Alec has a soulmate. And we're neighbors, we're not going to be mean."

"I'm sorry, baby," Andi apologized, and she kissed Pollyanna's head before signaling with her fingers that she was watching Alec, all where the mousy girl couldn't see.

"Welcome to the soulmate dorm," Albany said with a smile, holding out a hand for me to shake. "I'm not a soulmate myself, I just come up here to hang out with the girls, so you'll probably see a lot of me." She let go of my hand and tipped her chin, looking up at Alec's head above mine, only barely crooking her eyebrow at him. "Alec."

Her one worded greeting needed no explanation.

"Albany," Alec responded, his hand sliding around my waist as he pulled me closer to him. "Ladies, this is my soulmate, Jaz. She's just returned to Highborn."

Albany's eyes flitted back to me with a welcoming smile. "Oh yeah, I've seen you around. My sister told me you trashed the potions room when the teacher was being a little shit."

"Returned?" Pollyanna asked as Alec's words finally hit her. Her tiny mouth scrunched up in thought, making her look even more adorable. "Did you go to Shadowhaven before now?"

Andi clicked her tongue and sighed at her soulmate. "Babe, she's the necromancer. Weren't you paying attention when we were talking about it the other day?"

Pollyanna sobered into a pout as she tried to remember, but then she brightened up like someone had switched a light back on. "Are you guys coming with us tomorrow?"

"Coming with?" I tilted my head up to look at Alec. He apparently was also in the dark about what she meant because he shrugged at me.

"We're all going on a field trip to a human city," Pollyanna squealed, tilting forward on her heels and clapping her hands together. Andi grinned at her, clearly infatuated with her mousy soulmate. "You can go with the group, or do something on your own. Either way, I can't wait!"

"Neither can we," Alec offered with a smile. "If you'll excuse—" Andi politely shoved us aside and the three girls waltzed right into our apartment without another word.

"Ohh!" Pollyanna exclaimed, turning in a delicate circle and staring at everything all at once. "So pretty!"

"It looks just like our room, Polls," Andi pointed out, sticking her unimpressed hands into her pockets.

Trying to remain calm in front of them, I hurriedly stood in the hall doorway and looked over my shoulder at the bathroom door where I saw Pierce peeking out of it. Gilbert was behind him, and he gave me a comforting smile before Pierce shut the door.

"Yes, rooms are fascinating," Alec pronounced, coming to stand beside me and appearing much more casual than I felt.

A wary Albany was watching us as the other two girls were marveling over our kitchenette, which, as Andi reminded her again, looked just like theirs. "Sorry if we caught you two off guard."

"Not to worry, we just haven't had a chance to put our things away yet, so if you'll just stay in here, the bedroom is rather a mess," Alec said smoothly.

"What, are you afraid we'll see your dildo collection or something?"

"*Albany!*" Pollyanna admonished as she shut the oven door and straightened in a huff. "I'm so sorry, Alec and Jaz. We'll come back another time when these girls *remember their manners.*" She stormed out, pulling Albany along with her, and Andi followed, stopping beside the front door.

"Polly can be a bit intense with the manners thing," she explained as Pollyanna's lecture could be heard retreating down the hall.

"I can see why you find her so endearing," Alec responded. "Just like I do with my Jaz here."

Andi's smile grew and she eyed Alec with a growing respect. "Catch you later, Claus." She shut the door behind her, making Alec and myself deflate as we let out the breath we'd been holding.

"What dildo collection?" Pierce asked from the bathroom. "Also, Gilbert put his hand through my nuts."

"It was an *accident!*" Gilbert hissed. "I said I was sorry!"

The bathroom door swung open and Pierce strode out, holding his shoes in his hands.

"I'll show you my dildos if you show me yours," Pierce said huskily, his eyes burning into me with their intensity. He definitely still made me nervous, but in a good way, and it was amplified with the knowledge that the four of us were alone in our new apartment.

Staring at a spot on the light blue walls, I straightened the waist of my dress to hide my shaking hands. "Now that we're alone, I realize that you're all looking at me like I'm a jar of cheese sauce." I gulped and tried to phrase my words properly, so I didn't sound like I was rejecting them. Not that I *didn't* want them all to throw me against the bed until it looked like a crime scene under a black light, but I was still unsteady about everything.

"You go and unpack your things in the bedroom, darling," Alec prompted, running a hand through his tousled locks. "Pierce, help me in the kitchen."

As Pierce passed him, the warlock motioned for Gilbert to follow, and he gave me a smile once all three boys were in the living room, waving his hand to encourage me so I'd go into the bedroom. Dropping my eyes, I turned and did just that, shutting the door behind me.

ALEC'S LITTLE BLACK BOOK

The giant bed in our bedroom was practically a planet, and as I stared at it, despite my inner turmoil, I pictured being on top of the sheets with Alec and Pierce wrapped around me, and Gilbert hovering nearby. The thought was electrifying, having all three of my lovers at the same time. My pulse beat faster with both fear and anticipation.

How did one juggle three people, especially when one of them was a fucking ghost?

Goddess, buckle up. I'm about to ask a ton of inappropriate questions.

Our bags were beside a *'his and her'* dresser, and I picked up my coffin backpack to place it on the bed before I unzipped it. Everything I owned was inside that bag, barring a few things still at my mom's house, accomplished with an extension spell.

With it open, I cast a simple spell to bring a few things out, and the room became a flash of colors as my clothes, books, and trinkets flew from the bag to hover above me like a curtain. I sent the books to rest atop the dresser, the underthings and pyjamas to inside some of the drawers, and my dresses to the wardrobe that stood beside the bed. Then I sent everything else back inside the bag before placing it next to my books on the dresser.

Alec had one bag as well, but I discovered it wasn't extended and instead had all of his things laid out and visible, like an Ordinary human bag. I took out his small clothes and put them in the opposite side of the dresser, leaving the middle drawers empty, then I hung his suits up in the wardrobe next to my dresses, also leaving space to the side.

The bottom of the wardrobe had a detachable shoe rack that I brought out and put beside the bed. In our short time together, Pierce was meticulous about removing his shoes while inside Alec's family home, and I wanted to have a place for our shoes by the door. Plus, wearing shoes inside a house was the best way to get dirty floors, and I was not going to keep dragging out the magical mop every day.

Finished unpacking, I bent to put Alec's empty bag

under the dresser as the door opened, and whoever had walked in was getting an eyeful of my ass, not that any of my lovers would complain about that.

"How's it going?" Pierce asked, and I turned to see him standing with the doorknob in his hand, his eyes definitely moving up from my butt.

I stuck my hand into my coffin bag and brought out some lip-gloss that I applied before slipping it into my dress pocket. "I've got our stuff unpacked, mostly. I usually just keep everything in my bag. It's easier. But I left some drawers empty and there's extra room in the wardrobe for your stuff. The wardrobe had a shoe rack and I'm going to move it to the front door for our shoes." I stopped talking because Pierce had gone very still, staring at me from across the room with an unreadable expression. "No on the shoes?"

One corner of his mouth curved, and he looked down at the floor when a sweet smile overtook his features. He flicked his eyes back up to me under a curtain of his perfect lashes, and that grin of his had my stomach flying out of my body. "You made space for me." I wasn't sure how he felt about it, despite his smile, and was starting to worry I'd done something wrong when he crossed the room and took my wrists in his hands. "You didn't have to do that."

"But you live here," I noted, and he silenced my fears with a deep kiss to my lips, gently capturing my mouth in a way that heated my entire body, and it wasn't only desire that I was feeling. There was something else creeping up on me from Pierce's delicate, slow kisses. Something warm and fragile that made me feel like smiling for hours. His fingers took my chin as he slipped his tongue into my mouth, and desire won over whatever I'd been feeling.

"Everything okay in here?" Alec interrupted, but Pierce kept kissing me when I tried to move away, his fingers on my chin ensuring I wouldn't be able to get loose.

My dominant boy. Still needed to learn how Jaz likes to play, it seems.

I got free by putting my hand on his erection and he hissed, breaking our embrace. We shared a playful look, a test of wills that neither would win, but we'd definitely have fun along the way.

"I'll take care of this," Alec said. Turning my head, I watched him pick up the shoe rack from beside the wardrobe and take it out of the bedroom, as if he'd read my mind.

Pierce took advantage of my distraction and dove into my exposed neck, kissing and nibbling on my skin, and my moan was much louder than I'd intended it to be. By the goddess, how would I ever survive with him in wolf form all day? I needed him in this form, the one that I could kiss and hold, and yes, fuck. Priorities.

"Pierce," Alec called, back in the doorway again, and the Lycan straightened with a sigh, tucking a strand of my curls behind my ear. "It's ready."

I instantly noticed a shift in their behavior. It was plainly obvious despite my limited time with them, and my eyes squinted with suspicion, but I allowed Pierce to take my hand and lead me back to the kitchen area.

I first noted that Alec had indeed placed the shoe rack by the door. He'd removed his shoes and put both his and Pierce's on one of the rows. I did a double take as I noticed another pair of shoes on the rack below Pierce's, shoes that were partially transparent. A quick look at Gilbert, who wasn't hovering as he usually did and instead was firmly standing on the ground, showed he wasn't wearing his boots, and his ghostly feet were bare. We shared a smile and I slipped off my flats, sending them to the rack with a spell.

"Well, now that we've got that done," Alec announced, placing his hand on one of the chairs where his jacket lay across the top. He took off his tie as well, laying it on the jacket, and he unbuttoned the top button of his shirt. Seeing his exposed throat made me want to kiss and nibble it just as Pierce had done to me. "Jaz, sit, please." Pierce pulled my chair out for me and helped push it in when I'd sat down. Gilbert sat across from me, still with his adorable smile, and Pierce joined Alec at the kitchen counters.

"This is different," Gilbert noted as he rested his transparent hands on the table. I took a moment to marvel at his progress of being able to do that before I answered.

"I've never had my own place before. I mean, not that this is really the same thing." My eyes trailed around the large room to take in the couch, coffee table, and the rug on the wood floor. It looked like an Ikea catalogue. Alec approached, leaning over to put a plate in front of me, and he brushed his lips over my forehead. "I thought we were supposed to go to the dining hall?"

"For dinner, yes," Pierce noted as he brought two other plates to the table and placed them in front of the empty chairs. "This is lunch." Alec kissed my forehead again before sitting at my left, and Pierce sat down on my right.

In the short time they'd had while I was unpacking, my lovers had cooked up some homemade mac and cheese with bits of hamburger meat mixed in. I smelled garlic and onion, along with several types of cheeses, and my mouth started watering before I'd even picked up my fork.

I slumped back into my chair, clutching my hands firmly in my lap under the table, still staring at Gilbert. "What did you talk about in here?" Gilbert shut his eyes and sighed like he knew this was coming, and it only further served to confirm my thoughts. "You're all acting weird, I want to know what happened. Did you warn Pierce off me again, Alec? I'm not going to think that's cute if you keep doing it."

Alec rubbed his hand across his forehead and put his fork down. "No, I didn't. Not in the way you're thinking."

"I *told* you," Pierce admonished, but he didn't appear to be pleased about being right.

My warlock almost reached for my hand but reconsidered right before I would've slapped it away. "You are not okay right now. You told us that at my home, and on the train. The conversations the three of us have are not meant to micromanage you, because I know that's what you're thinking. We have to all be on the same page, that's what good soulmates do, Jaz."

I clenched my jaw and suddenly had to fight back the tears that pooled in my eyes. Part of me was humiliated that their actions were even necessary, but the other part appreciated their care on my part. Regardless, my face burned under their gazes, and both Alec and Pierce moved closer to me at the sight of my turmoil, but I didn't want them at that moment.

Gilbert, having stayed silent this entire time, ghosted through the table until he was in front of me, and I threw my arms around his neck, his transparent body as solid as I was with no effort on my part. His arms went around my back, causing a delicious chill to run over me.

"We would never do anything to hurt you," Gilbert assured me, his cold lips pressed against my temple. I could see Pierce's worry through my ghost's torso, and I knew that Gilbert was right.

"I'm sorry," I said quietly, gripping the folds of Gilbert's tunic in my hands. "I just can't stand to be controlled."

"Because of Candace?" Alec questioned, though it was clear he knew the answer. Gilbert unfolded my arms from him and guided me onto his lap as he took my seat. I was actually able to sit on him, and he put his cold arms around my waist, then handed me my fork.

"I'd rather not... discuss that," I hesitated, gripping my fork far too tightly.

As a response, Alec unbuttoned his cuffs and rolled his sleeves up until they were gathered in a sexy roll above his elbows. Goddess, have mercy on my thirsty soul.

"My sister died when I was young," he said once he was finished rolling up his sleeves like a slut. "I'm sure you wondered why I reacted so strongly when you were kidnapped. That's the reason. Her name was Luna. There are some days when I can't remember her face, it was so long ago when she died. I keep a photo of her in my wallet to remind me."

He reached into the pocket of his slacks, and brought

out a grey wallet with spells woven into the fabric. Opening it, he pulled out a small photo of a little girl. She had blonde hair and striking grey eyes that looked just like his. She couldn't have been more than eleven or twelve. I could see Lady Claus in her face too. Maybe that's why my future mother-in-law always looked so unhappy.

As I sat on Gilbert's lap staring at the photo, Pierce leaned back in his chair and slowly took the rubber band out of his long brown hair. "After we met, I asked my parents how they would feel if I mated with a witch." He gave a dry smile and raked his hands through his hair. "They told me if that happened to not bother coming home."

My throat constricted with unshed tears for both of them, but thankfully Alec said the words I couldn't find. "I'm sorry, Pierce. You don't have to say anything to them about us, you know we value all of our safety over honesty."

Pierce gave a half-shrug and his smile grew more desperate, like he was trying to prove to us and himself that it didn't matter to him. "I've always been expected to be better. *Be more like your sisters, Pierce*. They're mated, have children, built strong packs. You're the man, you have to be better than them. I never quite appreciated downplaying my sisters' accomplishments like that, but *Appa*, my dad, didn't care about my feelings on the subject. Kind of liberating in a way, not having to worry about their opinion."

"Isn't that the truth," Alec agreed dryly, folding his arms over his chest.

I took Gilbert's hand in mine, enjoying the rush of goosebumps that came from the coldness of his skin. "And your pack still doesn't know?"

"Definitely not," Pierce answered quickly. "One of my sisters is part of my pack, and she will absolutely tell my parents. Then there'll be a power play, fighting for dominance, blah blah blah. Though, Gia was like that all the time anyway. She'll just enjoy it more now."

I went quiet, staring down at my plate. So much sacrifice on my part from both of them. Alec would be giving up his estate, money, status, all for me. And Pierce would probably lose his entire family. I never wanted them to lose things on my behalf.

"How about you, ghosty?" Alec said to my chilly companion. "Got anything to confess?"

"Still can't remember my name. Or my life. The only thing to confess is... any second now." Before I could ask, I suddenly dropped down to the chair as Gilbert's body lost its solidity. "Sorry, darling." Lifting myself up, I rubbed at my sore ass cheek and looked down to see Gilbert's legs were sitting through mine. "That was fun while it lasted though. Let's go for some boob action next time."

I rolled my eyes and picked up my fork. "Okay, Alec 2.0." My mac and cheese was surely cold by now, but as I stared at it with their words swirling around in my head, I felt just safe enough to open up. They had earned that much, and after all, I'd long since made up my mind to trust them, even if my execution was delayed. "Candace used to be my friend, before I lost my magic. Hilary, my ex-best friend, grew up with me, and Candace let us into her group. It started out okay, she clearly expected us to do whatever she wanted but we went along with it, thinking it was normal to be someone's lackey. It got worse, though, to the point where Candace dictated what I wore, how I acted, who I spent time with. But then Taylor happened."

I took a sip of my water and wished it was coffee, or tequila.

"Taylor is a trans man that I met when I was fifteen, and we instantly liked each other. We dated for a few months, but I had to keep it secret because all of our relationships had to be approved by Candace. Taylor's grades slipped and he had to leave school. It's a good thing he did, I've told myself over the years, because I lost my magic soon after that, and everyone abandoned me that day. I haven't heard from him since then."

"Competition," Alec muttered under his breath. "Alright, out with it, I would like to know who all of your past lovers were."

"*Alec*," Pierce chastised through gritted teeth. "Inappropriate. She doesn't have to tell us that."

I knew Alec wouldn't be able to drop it with his jealous streak rearing its new and annoying head, so I rolled my eyes and spilled the beans. "Only Taylor. We had sex once before he left. Then it was Pierce, and you. That's it."

Pierce's eyebrows raised in surprise. "For real?"

"For real," I repeated, and I pinned Alec's steel eyes as I rested my fist on my chin. "How about you, romance king. Where's your little black book?"

He worked his mouth a bit before reaching over to where his coat was and he produced a little notebook. I'll admit, my mouth dropped open because I was partially joking. "Before I give you this..." His eyes flicked to Pierce and Gilbert before landing back on me. Was he *blushing*? "I expect your opinion of my reputation to stay the same." With that, he pressed the little black book into my hands.

Well. Here we are. I was about to discover all of Alec's sexual exploits. This book held all the names of all the people he'd fucked, sucked, twiddled, and kissed.

I didn't even want to open it.

Don't get me wrong, I knew he was a man whore. I knew there had to be pages upon pages of names in there. It just didn't matter. He belonged to me now.

Every single list in there would end with my name, and that's how they would stay forever.

I handed the book to Pierce and he studied my expression carefully. "I don't want to read it. I'll know what to think from your face."

The Lycan flipped the book open, Gilbert's fingers just barely ran through my hair, and Alec's hand came to rest on my knee under the table. Pierce did his best to remain expressionless as he flipped through a few pages. He stopped at one and his eyebrows slightly raised again, his mouth visibly twitching as he fought off whatever emotion he was feeling. His eyes then flicked up to Alec's and they stared at one another for a few tense moments.

"Really?"

Alec's hand squeezed my knee. "Really. Go to the next one."

Pierce did, and this time he couldn't hide his smile before he flipped the book and held it out to me.

The page read:

Lovers that I care about.
Jonas Mitchell.
Jasmine Neck.

The first name was faded like he'd written it a long time ago, and my name was fresh and new.

"That's really the only page that matters," Alec said, his voice tender and timid, and his thumb running along the edge of my knee. "How about you, wolf boy?"

Wordlessly, Pierce held up his hand with all five fingers sticking up. He wiggled his thumb and grinned at me. "That's you, baby. The best one, and the only one I care about."

"Still no idea, can't contribute," Gilbert added. "But if I had to guess, *definitely* more than Alec. I am utterly irresistible."

I felt his ghostly lips on my shoulder, but when I reached back to ruffle his dark hair, I couldn't feel anything. We'd used up our daily cuddle ration, it seemed. Deflated from that, I snapped my fingers and our food started steaming with warmth again.

"Thank you for making lunch, guys," I praised as I handed Alec his book back. His little pink fairy Armadillo was nestled in his shirt collar against his neck. I reached a finger over to Astella and scratched at her little fluffy head.

"You don't want to see? You're certain?" Alec asked, holding the book up.

Standing, I leaned over him and tilted his chin up to give him a gentle but commanding kiss. "Nope."

While keeping eye contact with me, the book floated up above Alec's hand and he snapped his fingers, incinerating the book into embers that lit up his features with orange light, and then it was gone like it never existed.

I smiled at him and flicked a bit of ash away from me. "You might regret doing that if you can ever convince one of them to suck your dick."

"Mmm," Alec mused, leaning up to me for another kiss, his stubble scratching against my skin. "That's true." Pierce made a gagging sound and Gilbert sighed like a disappointed parent. "Sit," Alec ordered, lifting his hand behind me to smack my ass, and I squealed before narrowing my eyes at him. "Eat." Still squinting at him, I sat down and Gilbert floated back to the empty chair across from me.

We tucked into the mouthwatering food, and once we were finished, I got up to make some coffee. I was stopped by shouting coming from the outside hallway just before someone pounded on the door.

"Guys!!!" a voice called out, sounding suspiciously like our new friend, Pollyanna. "You have to come see!"

5

I SWEAR I WON'T TELL

Alec immediately stood and started picking up our empty dishes as Pierce shifted into a wolf and Gilbert disappeared into the ceiling, leaving me to answer the door. A breathless Pollyanna stood in the hallway, Andi shutting a door further down the hall and approaching as she ran a hand through her short hair.

"OMG, Jaz, Alec, hurry up or you'll miss it!" Pollyanna squealed, jumping up and down, making her long hair fly into my face.

I coughed and spit out one of her hairs that had landed on my mouth. "Ugh, is that what it's like for you with my hair, Alec?" He'd grabbed my bag from the bedroom and handed it to me as Pierce came out into the hallway, then Alec guided me out as well so he could lock our apartment door.

"Yes," he answered simply, booping me on the nose, and Pierce bumped into me, knocking me into Alec's arms.

"Is this going to be a habit with you?" I ground out as I glared at the wolf.

"Cute doggie!!" Pollyanna exclaimed and she gave Pierce ear scratchies, making him pant happily. "Jealous. My familiar is a mouse. She just wants to eat cheese all day, she thinks I'm boring."

"Stupid mouse," Andi grumbled, her mouth pinched in anger that anyone would dare to dislike her soulmate.

"What are we going to look at?" Alec asked them, and Pollyanna jumped up again with her sunshine filled grin.

"Shadowhaven is here! Come, come, come!" She hopped up to me and grabbed my hand, dragging me to the stairs until we were out of the lobby and outside under the blinding sun.

"Polls," Andi shouted as she trotted to catch up to us, grabbing Pollyanna's hand away from my arm. "Baby, let her walk on her own."

Pollyanna hugged her soulmate and started tugging her along instead, throwing over her shoulder, "Hurry up, Jaz!"

Alec's footsteps picked up until he was putting his

arms around me and he took off in flight, holding me close to him as I shrieked and wrapped myself around him.

"A shame I can't see your skirt going up right now," he remarked mid-flight, and I smacked his back with my hand before we landed dramatically in the front courtyard. My skirt was billowing, my long curls were flying everywhere, and there was a deep flush on my cheeks when Alec pulled me closer to him by my waist and claimed my mouth with his demanding lips.

"Show off," someone complained, and I turned away from Alec to see an entire crowd of people staring at us.

Piss.

The one who had commented was Candace Cauldron, looking perfect in her designer witch clothes, and she shot daggers at me for existing.

"They're here!" Pollyanna exclaimed once she'd caught up to us. Pierce was by my side so quickly, he bumped me again in his eagerness to get between me and the crowd around us, just in case someone wanted to hurt me.

"Hey, Alec," a tall redheaded guy said, biting down on his fingernail as he appraised my soulmate.

"Chase," Alec said without missing a beat and I rolled my eyes.

"Ahh, there you all are," Professor Halace said as she appeared in the courtyard with her snooty gorgeous face glaring right at me. Of course, she had to be here.

A tall warlock with a thick beard stepped away from the crowd and approached her, his skin turning pinker as he got closer. "Selene, lovely to see you again."

She barely looked at him. "You were supposed to arrive on Friday. We don't have the dorm ready yet."

"Apologies, there was a case of the Willies in Shadowhaven village and we didn't want to take a chance on the children catching it."

Halace's bored expression turned to surprise and sympathy as she put a shocked hand to her chest. "Oh dear, that's horrible! I hope there isn't an outbreak. That would be awful."

I made a face at the idea of a Willies outbreak. She was right, it would suck.

"Why is Shadowhaven here, anyway?" Candace complained loudly. "We don't need second rate witches stinking up our school."

I stepped out from the shade of Alec's body so I could glare at her. "You know what, Candace, stick it up your ass, no one asked you."

"Language," Halace threw over her shoulder, but didn't deem us worthy of turning around.

I flipped Candace off and leaned my elbow against Alec's shoulder. Pierce's furry body brushed against my leg as he stepped between us and her, his menacing growl so loud, it echoed around the courtyard.

Candace looked like she was about to piss herself.

"*Miss Neck*," Halace shouted at me, and Pierce instantly stepped back, his ears flattening as he bowed his head towards me. "Keep your familiar under control or it's a demerit."

I pet Pierce's giant head and smiled sweetly at her. "Good doggie."

"Demerit."

"*Worth it.*"

"Alec," the bearded teacher warlock addressed with a smile, though not in the same way as the cute redhead had. "Lovely to see you again."

"Claus, you should go with the Professor and help the Shadowhaven students get settled in the guest dormitory. We hadn't assigned an escort yet, but since you used to attend, you're a good choice."

Halace's face booked no refusals, so Alec kissed my forehead and helped guide the group inside the school. While they were filing into the front doors, Candace and her friends approached me, their arms folded over their chests in what they thought was an intimidating pose, but really it just looked like they were trying to show more cleavage.

Candace leaned into me and I could smell something phallic on her breath. "You won't be able to hide behind

Alec forever, *witch*." Pierce snapped his enormous jaws at her and she jumped away with a scream before scowling even more at me.

"You're right, but that's okay, because I don't need him to protect me from you. You should think more about finding someone to protect you from *me*." I flipped her off again and grabbed Pierce's scruff before mixing in with the Shadowhaven crowd and going inside the school building, veering off to the right where the staircase was.

As we passed one of the janitor's closets, Pierce pulled my skirt with his teeth and dragged me into the open door, shutting it with his tail once we were both inside.

He was shifted into his human form and kissing me before I'd caught my breath. "I swear to god," Pierce muttered, his head dipping into my shoulder where he nibbled on my skin until a moan hissed through my teeth. "I'm going to go insane. I can't hold you in my wolf form. And I definitely can't wring that bitch's neck in wolf form either. If she lays a finger on you, I'm going to bite her fucking head off."

Even though he was taking about decapitating the worst girl in school, I was so turned on by him defending me, I couldn't think straight. "That's the hottest thing anyone has ever said to me," I told him, letting out a gasp when he cupped my breasts with both hands.

"Being here will be worse than Alec's house. If you're not in my arms from the time I wake up until I fall asleep at night, it's like having my leg cut off."

"Or a different appendage, more like," I said against his lips, sliding my hand right over his pants and fondling his hard cock. The Lycan responded by lifting my chin with his finger and taking my lips in his own, claiming me forcefully and tenderly at the same time, only allowing me to break away for air when I was so aroused, I felt dizzy.

Pierce grabbed my dress, pulled it over my hips and slipped his fingers into my panties, effectively ruining any attempt I'd had at staying quiet. My clitoris was so swollen and wet, my hips jerked when his fingers brushed over it, and I pressed further into his body for more.

Through my haze, I did fully remember we were skirting danger by doing this where someone could walk in at any moment. Even with Pierce's finger doing delicious things to my clit and making my body thrum with heat, I didn't want to put him at risk. Gasping, I tugged at Pierce's shirt and pulled us to behind one of the shelves in the small room, enough where if someone came in, they wouldn't see us.

"I'm going to make you fucking come with all those people outside the door," Pierce breathed in my ear.

Fuck.

He pushed me against the wall, hungrily kissing my lips, and used his knee to slightly spread my legs. The finger on my clit slowly circled it, my wetness only adding to the sensation, and when I threw my head back and moaned loudly, Pierce firmly clamped his other hand over my mouth.

"Ssh," he warned, and delicately traced the top of my clit, making me want to scream. I whined and met his eyes, his firm, possessive stare making me even wetter. Him looking at me like that with his finger rubbing my clit was sending me into a head spin. "I never thought I could want someone as much as I want you. All day long the scent of your arousal wraps around my brain, and I can't tell you what it does to me." As he spoke, he went back to tracing all around my clit, avoiding the swollen nub to drive me insane.

My legs started to tremble, my body straining for more. Pierce was intentionally keeping me from tipping over the edge, drawing out my pleasure as long as possible with those slow, torturous movements. Inhaling sharply, I hit the point of no return, dipping my head forward with his hand still muffling my moans that were growing louder. He stopped playing nice, and used two fingers to firmly swirl my clit, bringing enough pleasure that my throat felt hoarse from my groans, and I knew I'd scream... any... second... *oh god*.

Pierce's fingers pressed harder, and I couldn't breathe

for a few precious seconds, when he whispered into my ear, "*You're mine.*"

My orgasm ripped through me, and my muffled scream under his hand went on and on as he pulled every last dredge out of me with his fingers until I went limp. His strong arms came around me, holding me against him and keeping me from falling as my legs had been turned to jelly.

"My beautiful Jaz," he whispered to me, running his fingers through my hair. He sighed then, making me tense against his shoulder.

"You'll have to jerk yourself off," I told him hoarsely. "I can't move my fingers."

He chuckled, bumping me slightly. "That's okay, I will just fuck you senseless tonight. It's about time Alec saw how hard I can make you come."

I snorted and set my feet firmly on the ground again. "If that's what you're all going to play at, I'm going to die of exhaustion before there's a winner."

Pierce lifted me up in his arms, his face level with my neck, and he looked up at me with that intensity again, making me shiver all over. "You'll come for us and you'll like it."

"Bossy," I said with a grin, and leaned down for a sweet kiss before holding his head close to me and feeling his hot breath on my neck.

My wolf set me down and brushed some of my hair

back before giving me another kiss. "I like your cheeks flushed like that," he noted huskily. "It's very clear someone just gave you an orgasm. They'll all think it was Alec, and no one will know it was me."

"You're going to do this every day, aren't you?" I asked with a raised eyebrow, and he nodded brightly. "Mkay, back to wolf form. Orgasms make me hungry."

He gave one regretful sigh before shifting to a wolf, then he came back to rub his head against me for ear scratchies. With me distracted, he stuck his nose under my skirt, right on the damp spot of my panties. I squealed loudly at the feeling of his wet snout against my sensitive lady bits.

"Bad boy, Pierce!" I shouted as he emerged from my skirt with a toothy grin. "You're not allowed to put your nose there, you overgrown rug, we've been over this!" He snorted at me, his expression clearly reminding me that he'd had his face there already and I didn't complain. Well, if you count screaming at the top of my lungs not complaining. Glaring at the silver wolf, I pointed a finger to the door of the closet. "Out. No more crotch sniffing."

Putting a hand on his rump, I pushed him towards the door and it opened with a twist of my fingers until we were out in the entrance hall. I fluffed my hair out and hoped Pierce was wrong about my flushed cheeks when I spotted Alec standing on the other end of the hall talking to two people.

"There you are," Alec called to me, and the people turned to face me, both of them making my heart stop but for different reasons.

The first was my ex, Taylor.

The second was the fucking popstar, Aurora.

She was utter witchly perfection. Her figure was mouthwatering, her hair was long and silky, and her skin was so dark she was almost onyx. Her dress hugged every curve like it owed her money, and it showed enough cleavage to make a priest double take.

I was so busy staring at her, I completely forgot about Taylor. He smiled widely when I turned to him, and my fingers clutched Pierce's fur. He was still as beautiful as he'd always been, with his rich brown skin and honey brown eyes.

"Jasmine," he said warmly, and he left Alec's side to approach me for a hug that I reciprocated, trying not to stare at Alec over his shoulder, just in case he was glaring at me. "It's been so long, I've missed you a lot, sweetheart." I'd missed him too, I just knew how Alec would react if I said so.

"Yes, you and Jaz are acquainted," Alec piped up, and I tried not to roll my eyes as Taylor broke our hug. "Jaz is my soulmate. *Magicae equidem*." Right to the punch, jealous boy.

"Really?" Aurora said in pleasant surprise, looking from Alec to me with a smile.

Taylor met my shy gaze with a warm grin. "That's amazing, Jaz. I'm glad you have a soulmate. You're far too special for anything less." Wolf Pierce stepped in front of me and sat down between my feet. If Gilbert had been there, what would his jealous reaction be? Sticking his hand through Taylor's dick?

"I've been looking forward to meeting you for a long time, Jaz," Aurora told me with a hand on her hip, and she looked me over like Candace always did, only to smile warmly at me in approval.

"Aurora's my sister," Taylor explained with a sheepish grin.

"You—" My mouth popped open and I almost reached out to smack his arm. "Your sister is fucking *Aurora* and you *never told me*? Such a bad friend."

Aurora giggled at my ire and rested her hand on Taylor's shoulder. "In Taylor's defense, he kept it a secret as a favor for me. I didn't want his school years to be ruined when everyone found out about our connection."

I narrowed my eyes at Taylor and quirked my mouth to the side. "But I swear I won't tell," I sang ironically, and the three of us burst out laughing. Smoke pooled at our feet, coming from Alec's nostrils like a smoke machine, and flames flickered in his eyes. "Babe, you're on fire."

Alec tossed his head and the smoke disappeared. "Lovely to see you again, Aurora." Then he stomped out of the entrance hall and slammed the doors closed, making us all jump.

Aurora shook her head with a smile. "Same old Alec."

I tried hard not to react to *another* person having tupped my soulmate, especially with him off having a jealous fit over my ex-boyfriend. "You and he..." I waved my hand around and felt flushed over asking her that.

"Look at you, being all jealous," Taylor teased, bumping my leg with his foot.

"*Shut up*," I squeaked.

"Taylor, come on, now. Don't tease her." Aurora flipped back a lock of her long black hair and gave me a sympathetic smile. "Alec and I had a brief... liaison." Taylor rolled his eyes at her word choice. "We never had sex. It wasn't because we didn't want to, it was just Alec's choice. He said he'd do anything with me, except that. It's not something he does on a whim, he said. I know, it's shocking considering his reputation. I can't say I wasn't disappointed, but, still, I rode his face afterwards, so I can't complain."

"*Gross*," Taylor gagged, poking his sister in the side. "Keep that to yourself."

Knowing he hadn't banged her was a relief, even though I still felt jealous. I looked towards where Alec had gone and anxiously shifted my feet back and forth. "So why is Shadowhaven here?"

"They *said* it's for some workshops. Apparently a few of the Council members will be coming to teach them. But…" Taylor looked around to be sure we weren't being overheard. "Everyone knows it's because the Lycan packs are moving closer to our school. After what happened here with the Centaurs, everyone is a little jumpy."

"Unnecessary if you ask me," Aurora said under her breath. Why wasn't Alec back? I twisted my hands in Pierce's fur and tapped my foot on the stone floor. Aurora giggled at me. "Go after your boo, baby. We'll see you at dinner."

I hugged them both and ran out of the entrance hall.

6

DREAMING OF DILDOS

Pierce trotted beside me as we ran to the one place I knew Alec would be at. He was leaning against the iridescent blue greenhouse wall with his vape pen out and proud, taking a long drag before he noticed us.

"Where's your boyfriend?" he asked dryly, letting the smoke out of his mouth.

Sighing loudly, I crossed my hands over my chest. "You ate Aurora's snatch. I fucked Taylor. What was that conversation we had at lunch about if not to acknowledge that we've all come into this relationship with a history?"

"It was," he mumbled, looking away. "But I can't stop the white hot jealousy I felt when he touched you."

"I second that," Pierce added, suddenly shifted and

standing beside me. I almost chastised him, but we were definitely alone, and if anyone approached, we would have enough time for him to shift back. "I guarantee if Gilbert was here, he'd be raging. He can't stand for anyone else to have you. He still barely tolerates us, even if we do get along."

I walked across the grass and put my hands on Alec's cheeks, holding him in place so he had to look down at me with his cold steel eyes. "I belong to you. Say it."

An echo of smoke trailed out of his nose and he worked his jaw a few times. "You belong to me."

"The next time you forget that, I'll take a tip from Candace and make you jizz yourself every time you see me."

His eyes narrowed at me. "You wouldn't dare."

I smirked and crooked an eyebrow at him. "Oh, I would, cupcake." Pausing, my mouth watered at the thought of strawberry cupcakes with whipped icing. "I want cupcakes."

Alec quickly turned me around and slammed my back into the greenhouse wall, roughly claiming my mouth. He slipped his tongue between my lips until I was panting underneath him. "You are mine," he said, repeating Pierce's words from earlier. "I saw you coming from that closet with your cheeks flushed from an orgasm. I hated anyone else seeing you that way. It brought out the beast in me."

"Oh come on," I complained and quickly squeaked when Alec shoved his knee between my legs. "It wasn't *that* obvious."

"Oh, I can assure you, it was. And that's ignoring the fact that I cast a tuning in spell the instant I saw Pierce drag you into that closet. Was that his hand over your mouth or his cock between your lips? I admit the sounds are quite similar."

"You!" I got out before he took my lips again and lifted me up with his knee until my feet were dangling above the ground.

Alec took my bottom lip between his teeth and slowly let it go. "Panties off."

"Bossy," I retorted instantly, lifting my chin in challenge. "Ask nicely and I'll reward you."

He grunted and gave me a light kiss. "Please get on the ground and spread your deliciously sexy legs so I can put my face between them. I'm sure Pierce will love the show."

"True enough," Pierce agreed.

Footsteps came from around the corner, stopping that thought cold. Alec set me down and Pierce had just enough time to shift and stand next to me as Cole and his friends approached us.

"Oh look," I exclaimed with an eye roll. "It's a two for one special on Cauldrons today."

Alec's mouth pinched together at the sight of Cole,

and he drew me closer to him. "I was just about to enjoy my lovely soulmate, but if you're wanting to suck your classmates' dicks, Cole, we'll be on our way."

While Cole's friends jeered at me, biting their lips suggestively and making kissy faces, Cole stared down at Pierce who was practically melding with my side, he was standing so close to me, and a deep rumble was building in his chest that got louder when Cole looked back up at me.

"Nice wolf, Neck."

"Th…" I clamped my lips together just in case he was trying to trick me. It wouldn't have been the first time.

Alec used his hand on my side to tug me away, keeping himself between me and the boys. "Have fun sucking cock, gentlemen."

❦

Gilbert was waiting for us when we made it back to our apartment, and he beamed at me before seeing Alec and Pierce's faces as we removed our shoes. "Bad day?"

"My ex, Taylor, is here. He arrived with the group from Shadowhaven," I explained, flinching slightly in preparation for his explosion.

His eyes widened first, then his hands slowly balled

into fists that he hid in the folds of his tunic. "And did he touch you?"

"A hug," Pierce told him, and Gilbert nodded, his mouth pressed into a thin line as he approached me and tilted my chin up with a single transparent finger.

"That is all he shall get." He leaned down, making my stomach tighten before he gave me a single kiss on the lips, one that left no doubt as to who I belonged to. "You're *ours*. Every man on the planet could parade in front of you naked and it would not change that fact. Still though, I may have to reveal myself just to make sure all the boys here keep their hands to themselves."

"I'll admit," I breathed against his lips. "I wasn't into the possessive talk at first, but now. I think you *would* win against a piece of cake."

Gilbert grinned and picked me up, holding me above him so I could put my arms around his neck. Pierce put his hands on my back and Alec stood behind the ghost, watching me carefully.

"Just in case he drops you," he told me.

Gilbert's determined look left little room for doubt. "I won't drop her this time."

I ran my hands through his transparent hair and it almost felt real, but it left my fingers feeling like I'd stuck them in the freezer. "I was expecting you to rage about a boy touching me."

"I told you I'm evolving," he said with a smile. "But I

can bitch about it for a few minutes if you'd like. It would take little effort." He paused, grunted, and set me back on the floor a few seconds before I couldn't feel his arms on me. "See? I'm getting better at knowing when that will happen."

"It should be dinner soon," Alec said, meeting my eyes through Gilbert's torso.

Something buzzed and Pierce reached into his jeans pocket for his phone. He read the text he'd just gotten and started putting his shoes back on. "Sorry, everyone, I have to go take care of something." He swiped some of his hair from his eyes and folded me to him for a long hug that made my stomach twist.

"You're coming back, right?" I let slip before I could stop myself, but with the words hanging in the air I just held him tighter until his warmth spread all over me.

"I will always come back to you, Jaz," Pierce assured me.

"You'd fucking better. You owe me a hard fuck."

Pierce pulled me away from him and forcefully walked me back until I'd gone through Gilbert's body and was pressed against Alec's chest. The warlock locked me to him with his arms around my waist as Pierce took my neck in his hands and kissed me long and slow.

I wanted our kiss in Alec's arms to go on forever.

Finally, long before I was ready, Pierce stepped back

through Gilbert's body and gave me one firm look before leaving.

Alec tightened his hold on me and bent to kiss my head. "He'll be back, darling. Let's not worry, okay?"

I stayed quiet for a while, staring at the door and hoping he'd immediately return. "We can't hide him forever, Alec. What will happen if one day I give birth to a baby that looks nothing like you? A baby that shifts into a wolf."

"I told you I'm working on something. Trust in me, Jaz."

"Is it stopping the war?" I asked absently, clutching my fingers around his arms.

"I would want nothing more. But I will do what I can until then."

My energy levels were suddenly drained, and all I wanted was to be held by Alec and Pierce until I fell asleep. "I'm going to bed." Alec let me go and I walked to the bedroom, crawling on top of the giant bed and bringing one of the pillows to my chest. Then I shut my eyes and I let myself drift off.

※

HAVE YOU EVER HAD THAT DREAM WHERE YOU'RE naked, you're being chased, your legs can't move, and there's bagpipes playing off key in the background?

Fun stuff.

With all of that happening to me, I suddenly was hit with a dildo to the face.

"Witch!" someone shouted angrily.

"Rude!" I retorted, trying to twist to see who'd thrown the dildo at me when another one full on mollywhopped my nose. "Those had better be clean!" My frustration won over my frozen legs, and I pretended to be Alec, shooting off from the floor and hovering over everything. Now I could see who was throwing the dildos: a very angry centaur.

Theseus.

His face was twisted in anger, and he was raising another dildo when he noticed my lack of clothing. He clearly liked what he saw, but was pretending not to. "You're naked, witch."

I looked down at my perfect floating breasts and back at him. "Yeah, so what? Drink it in, pony boy." He tossed the dildo in his hand and I swirled to avoid it, watching it disappear into the void that was outside our little dream arena. "I don't remember taking acid, but I'm not going to complain about my dreams being more exciting for once."

Theseus somehow had another dildo, this one the size of my entire waist, and it would definitely leave a mark on my face if he didn't miss. "This isn't a dream, witch. This is hell, and you're my captor. I demand to be set free."

"Hitting me with dildos is a weird way to ask for a favor, but whatever."

"Suck on this!" Theseus shouted, and he launched the giant dildo at me. I moved to avoid it, but it followed me until it slammed into my stomach and tossed me out of the dream where I woke up in my bed and sat up with a hoarse gasp. Horse gasp, more like.

Alec mumbled something in his sleep and reached out for me, sliding his hand onto my bare thigh where my dress had ridden up. *"Tu vas bien, chérie?"*

Having no clue what that meant, I lifted his hand, kissed it, and tucked Alec back in under the blanket. "I'll be back," I whispered, just in case he was awake enough to hear me. I slid off the bed and grabbed one of the keys Alec had left out on the dresser. Alec rolled over in his sleep as I slid on one of my coats in the wardrobe, and I tiptoed to the front door and put my shoes on before leaving our apartment.

The air outside the soulmate dorm was freezing cold, and the grass crunched under my feet from a thin layer of frost that had settled over the lawn. I trotted as fast as I could so I wouldn't freeze to death before I got to where I was going, and when I finally stood in the dining hall entry way, I felt like death warmed over. My breath was visible in the cold hallway, and I worked to stop my chest from heaving. My fingers went to the neck of my coat to hold the seams together as if it would protect me from the room.

It still haunted me, that night at the dance when Theseus couldn't be saved. I still blamed myself for my inaptitude, my inability to do my damn job. I was trying so hard to move on, but guilt was a cruel mistress.

My feet felt frozen, like I was back in my dream, but I moved them forward across the stone floor, and didn't stop until I was sitting in the middle of the room, just off to the side, at that spot where the centaur had died.

The tiles looked perfect again, not a scratch or drop of blood on them. It was *wrong*. How could they just erase Theseus? You can fix the floor, you can rebuild the room, but can you pretend it never happened?

"Witch," a voice said, and I automatically flinched in preparation for another molly-whop, but nothing came, and I peeked an eye open to see the ghost of Theseus hovering above one of the tables. His long braids were floating around his ghostly blue chest, and he still looked as muscled and intimidating as he had when he was alive.

I scrambled up, my mouth popping open in shock, but all the words were stolen from my throat until one slipped out. "*Piss!*"

He looked puzzled at my response. "I am called Theseus. Have you forgotten?"

"No, I wasn't..." I rolled my eyes. "Do all centaurs have no sense of humor or is that just you?"

"I am surprised your mates allow you to speak to a man like that."

"Wooooow," I said, drawing the word out until it was as long as a clothesline. "There is so much to unpack from that, I'm going to run out of room. Let's skip it, because I'm too sleepy, and there's no coffee." Theseus' massive chest still looked like a buffet table I'd love to run my tongue all over, if I wasn't fully invested in my soulmates. He trotted up to me mid-air but seemed unable to touch the floor as Gilbert could. "First question, were you really in my dream?" He nodded. "Where'd you get the dildos from?"

"They were already there."

Heh.

"Mkay, so you're needing me to what, try to resurrect you again? I kinda need a body for that, and in case you haven't noticed," I said, spreading my arms to gesture at the empty room. "There's no body here."

"I would not chance a second try, as it would destroy any hope I have left," Theseus proclaimed eloquently, but also as dry as unbuttered toast. "Plus, I am not certain you can."

"You'd be right, but thanks for the confidence."

He grunted at me, the wet blanket version of rolling his eyes. "I am stuck at this school, I cannot leave the barrier. Whatever your warlock did to it only allows for your ghost mate to come in and out. It's probably better that way, considering what other spirits lurk out there, but I am unable to be comfortable while I am confined here."

"Sorry, but you're a little SOL asking me. I don't have the specialty to touch the barrier. Also, does said ghost mate know about you being here?"

"Naturally."

Gilbert, you transparent motherfucker.

"He has avoided me thus far, so please don't be harsh on him for it. I too have seen how much my death has affected you. He no doubt wished to spare you more pain."

My mouth dropped open again, and I was *so* glad my school activities thus far hadn't involved me being naked. "Okay, spying on me is *so* not cool. You try it again and I will clip your ghostly dick."

Theseus grimaced and shifted his legs from one hoof to the other. "Noted, witch." He wisely looked the other way to avoid my scowl. "I have gathered a few thoughts which I hope will aid your plight. I know my opinion can't count for much, considering I am a beast and you are a witch."

My face softened and I lowered my head. "I don't care about that." He was studying me carefully when I met his eyes. "Why are you offering me advice when you're the one who needs help?"

He rolled his shoulders in a half shrug. "That's fair enough. But still, I have never been one to keep silent if I think my perspective will aid."

I sighed and put my cold hands into my coat pockets. "Okay, Theseus. I will help you leave the barrier, and I'll accept whatever advice you'd like to give on how much I suck at being a necromancer."

He gave a dry chuckle and some of his long braids slid down his shoulder. "That's just it, witch. Maybe you should spend less time pouting, and more time learning."

"That sounds awesome, bruh. How about I just keep resurrecting people until it starts working? That would be *perfect*." I crossed my arms over my chest and kicked at the floor. "I'm never resurrecting again."

"And you feel this is the correct conclusion to draw?"

I turned to him, my eyebrows knitting together. "No other witch I know has reservations about their power, so clearly that means I should stop doing it. Right?"

"Hmm," he mused, looking away. "I think you're asking the wrong person. You need to ask someone who has no personal investment in whether or not you succeed. More importantly," he added. "Someone who understands exactly what's at stake when you dabble with life and death."

Sighing, I chewed on my lip until it started to hurt.

"Thank you, Theseus. I know I don't look like I appreciate the advice, but I do. When Alec wakes up, I'll ask him to let you out of the barrier, okay?"

The centaur nodded to me and took a few seconds to dip his eyes below my face. "Don't tell anyone I said this, but... I find myself regretting that you are no longer without clothes."

"Get the fuck out, Theseus."

7

THE DEMON FRANK

After Theseus fucked off, I sat on one of the dining tables for several hours, just staring at that spot on the floor. Whatever choice I made about my powers wouldn't be an easy one, but Theseus was right. I needed to ask someone who didn't care about me. Someone who hated what I was. There was only one individual who fit that bill, and I didn't look forward to conjuring up that demon again. And I mean literal demon.

With the school still quiet and empty, I easily made my way up to the divination classroom. Halace kept it neat and tidy, albeit she was a little dumb to leave her stuff out, so finding a crystal ball was embarrassingly easy. I set it on Halace's round desk atop a pretty tablecloth, and picked up a deck of tarot cards that were nearby before propping my feet up on the table.

The smoke inside the ball swirled around, waiting for my command of who to summon, but since I'd already touched it, I knew who I wanted would come eventually. I shuffled the deck around in my hands, removing a card here and putting it there, since I still couldn't shuffle them properly. The Lovers card ended up on top after a while at the same moment that the crystal ball vibrated, announcing my summon had worked.

"Necromancer," the demon greeted.

"Oh shit, whaddup, demon," I answered it, continuing to shuffle the cards.

"Didn't think you'd be back. I thought my warning had been well received."

I scoffed and plucked out a card to place on the table beside the ball. "I'm not a great listener, sorry to disappoint."

The demon paused, the smoke swirling around in the ball turning a tint of green. "And I didn't frighten you either. Puzzling."

"Not that I enjoy giving you satisfaction, but you did, just a little."

"Only a little?" He sounded disappointed.

"Don't be like that. When we met, I was basically eternally shell shocked, nothing got through to me. It's not personal."

He clicked his tongue. "And yet you're back here, speaking to me. Why is that, necromancer?"

Sighing, I put another card onto the table. "First off, I'd like to know who I'm speaking with."

"Hmm," he contemplated, sounding gleeful. "Guess I can't go with the father rouse again. Disappointing. I rather enjoyed that." I glared at the ball where he couldn't see. "I'm sure you're expecting someone famous, interesting, well-known."

"Swear to god, demon, if your name is Lucifer, I'm going to the demon portal to shove my foot up your ass."

He grunted at me. "You'll be pleased to know that I am not the king of hell. Good thing too, he's kind of an asshat."

"And you're not?" I whispered under my breath.

"I am the demon Frank."

I almost dropped the deck of cards. "Fr-... You're joking."

"I'm not."

Raising my eyebrows, I tilted my chair back a little. "I'm embarrassed to say that I was ever afraid of someone named *Frank*."

"Judgmental human," he grumbled. Growling to myself, I went silent, shuffling the cards as I had been, and not even looking at the crystal ball. Every so often I heard small noises coming from it, like Frank was starting and stopping himself from speaking. Finally, when I'd made several piles on the table and gathered them back up again, he sighed, drawing my attention back to the ball. "Are you still there?"

"I don't know, Frank. Awfully rude of you to be a little shit when a woman is letting you into her DMs."

"You called me," he pointed out in a growl. "And I can't be disconnected unless you stop touching the ball."

I tilted my head at the glass and grinned. "I'm not touching it."

Frank let off a string of curse words and then went deadly quiet, so much so that I almost asked if *he* was there this time. "You've gotten more powerful," he stated with annoyance.

"Kind of a necessity when you're dating a ghost. The more powerful I get, the more we can touch." Frank went silent again. "I'm working up to being able to fuck him. Then you'll really be impressed."

"I really won't." I rolled my eyes and tossed the cards onto the table, folding my hands over my stomach. "And it's really lucky I'm not your dad with you being so open about fucking a ghost. That's disgusting, by the way."

"Don't kink shame me, Frank. Plus, you're the one who pretended to be my dad in the first place."

He grumbled and sighed again. "Just ask me your question and let me get back to what I was doing. Some of us have lives, you know."

I bit back a comment about what a demon could *possibly* have going on that was so interesting. "Frank. I'm going to level with you." Sighing, I pressed my fingertips to the bridge of my nose and inhaled deeply. "I tried to resurrect a centaur and it didn't work. I conjured his spirit, brought it to his body, and nothing. I know you hate what I am, I shouldn't exist, blah blah. Let's get past that, shall we?"

Frank was silent again, and I felt sick to my stomach at what his answer would be. "You *shouldn't* exist," he reiterated.

"Yep, heard it. And if I can't resurrect someone properly then... I think you're right."

"Listen," Frank began, making me put my feet down so I could bend over the ball. "I'm not saying I like that you exist. Scourge on the earth, I believe is how I put it. But... and don't you *dare* tell anyone I said this. I think the fact that you're taking this so seriously is a good thing. Questioning yourself when it involves life or death is exactly how you should feel. Now, that's all I'm saying, and you'd better hang up this call or else I will *really* make you afraid."

"How's life with a micro-penis, Frank?" Before he could shout at me, I touched the ball again and the connection was broken.

Even as the smoke disappeared inside it, I stayed sitting at the desk. I couldn't say I was resolved in either direction now. To resurrect, or not to resurrect? Who the fuck knew.

Standing, I stretched my tired limbs and left the divination classroom, going all the way down to the bottom of the staircase. Gene Pendragon was about to go inside the dining hall when I arrived behind him. He noticed me with a yawn as he cleaned his glasses using the corner of his shirt.

"Hey, Neck," he said with his mouth still open from the yawn. I nodded to him and he came closer to me. "Tell Alec we miss him at Crypts and Casters."

"I will." I went towards the front doors, but he stopped me with a hand to my elbow.

"Neck. Are you okay?" I sighed and turned back to him, trying to smile, but seriously, how many people were going to ask me that? "I know you've been upset about what happened after the centaur raid."

"No doubt the entire school is talking about it."

He chuckled at me. "They are, but you've always been easy to read. For me at least, but some people are easier to read than others."

My eyebrows knit together as I studied Gene's gentle, sleepy expression. "You're empathic? How come I didn't know?"

He shrugged with a smile. "You never talked to me. It's fine, people usually don't. Telling them I'm a level 80

Paladin in Final Fantasy XIV doesn't exactly have people clamoring to be my friend."

I bit back a retort about him being a nerd because maybe that wasn't such a bad thing.

"I remember what you were like in middle school," he continued in a sleepy haze. "You were different back then. You didn't really belong with anyone, which makes sense now. I'm not surprised Alec's your soulmate, he was always the same way. You're really good for Alec. I hope you know that. I've never seen him this happy before. But to be fair, he's good for you too."

"You're being a little creepy, Gene."

He snorted and adjusted his glasses. "Sorry. Girls rarely let me talk this long." He gave me the Vulcan salute and started towards the dining hall.

"Hey, Gene." He paused, turning back to me. "We'll be at your next game, if that's okay. When is it?"

"Saturday," he answered, appearing a bit more awake. "Catch you later, Neck."

I left the building and walked back to the soulmate dorm, sitting down on the cold front step. My throat had just started hurting from the chilly air when my giant silver wolf finally appeared. He saw me waiting for him and broke off into a run across the grass. I opened the front door of the dorm and raced up the stairs with him behind me, fumbling to unlock our door, but he was shifted back to a human before I could take my key from the keyhole.

Pierce pushed me against the door and feverishly kissed me like we'd been apart for weeks, his hands roughly pulling my shirt up so he could cover my cold breasts with them. I let out a noisy moan that he smothered with his lips. "Ssssh," he told me, blowing against my mouth and squeezing my breasts in the same breath.

"Jaz?" a sleepy voice called down the hall. Pollyanna was standing in her doorway wearing a bunny rabbit onesie with the hood pulled over her head.

"*Fuck*!" I clicked the key into place, opened our door, and shoved Pierce inside as Pollyanna approached me, stretching and yawning.

"Who was that?" she asked mid-yawn.

I nervous planted myself against the door. "Umm… Alec."

She wrinkled her nose at me and picked at the corner of her eye. "Alec isn't that short."

Fuck. "I think you're asleep, Polly."

She gave a half-laugh and her eyes drooped. "That's probably true." With another yawn, she pat me on the shoulder and turned to go back to her apartment. "See you later, Jaz."

Fucking shit in a handbasket.

I stayed leaning against the door for a few moments until my heart stopped beating out of my chest. The door suddenly opened and I fell backwards into Pierce's arms. He twisted us around, closing the door behind us, and crushed me to him in a hug.

"I'm so sorry," he said, switching back and forth between Korean and English, but repeating the same apology over and over. "I'm being careless, and it's going to get me caught. First with the train, then the janitor's closet, and now this. Maybe I should just stay in here all day until you come back."

"No!" I wrapped my hand around the back of his head and pulled him closer to me. "I don't want you alone."

He gave a strangled sigh, resting his chin on my shoulder. "I have to keep you safe by keeping myself safe."

If I could've hugged him harder and fused our bodies together, it might've soothed the panic inside me, but as it was, I felt like I was flying apart.

Pierce gently pried me from him and ran his hand down my cold cheek. "You're freezing, are you okay? How long were you outside? You'll get sick if you stay in the cold like that, witch or no." My Lycan continued fussing over me, removing his shoes before kneeling in front of me to take my sandals off. "God, your feet are so icy. We should put some socks on you."

I was still terrified of him being discovered, but I realized it wasn't just his safety that was worrying me. I didn't want to live one day without him by my side, and that shook me right to my core. When had he become so important to me? I couldn't remember a shift from '*I'm not your mate*' to what I was feeling right then.

He looked up at me from where he knelt beside my feet, those gorgeous brown eyes of his shining in the early morning light. I stroked my fingers through his brown hair and marveled at how utterly beautiful he was.

I love you.

The words popped up into my thoughts and I inhaled sharply to drive them away. There was no way I could feel that yet. How long had we known each other? Two weeks? That was way too short a time to fall in love. And if I proclaimed something like that to him, only for him to be ripped away from me, I'd never recover.

Best to keep it to myself. For now.

Someone mumbled incoherently, and we turned to see Alec standing in the hallway, sleepily rubbing his eyes. Pierce had enough time to stand before Alec walked closer and put his arms around both of us. He leaned into me for a kiss on my lips, and switched to Pierce, only to be stopped with a hand pressed to his face.

"Nope," Pierce told him, and Alec grumbled before resting his head on mine.

"What fucking time is it," Alec asked, almost slipping into a different accent.

Pierce quickly checked his phone and allowed Alec to put his arm back around him. "About seven."

"Oh *for fuck's sake*, why am I conscious? Bed. Now." Alec tugged on our clothes and dragged us to the bedroom before he flopped onto the mattress in a swan dive, then he pressed a single finger to the bed beside him. "You. Here, witch."

"I'm not a puppy."

His angry tone was muffled by the blanket under his mouth. "If I have to speak more words, I'm going to give you a tongue lashing so severe, you won't be able to move until tomorrow morning."

"You say that like it would be a bad thing," I said under my breath.

He sighed and gave a slight whine. "Please."

How could I refuse Alec saying please?

Pierce and I shared a small smile before I climbed into the bed and laid down beside Alec who immediately folded me against him. Pierce came after me to cuddle my back, and he brought the blanket up to cover us. Lying between their warm bodies made me realize how cold I'd become being outside. I snuggled closer to Alec, and Pierce moved with me until there was no space between the three of us.

"Just how I like my threesomes," Alec whispered sleepily, and he laid a hand on my hip, his palm sliding across me so he could slip his finger into one of Pierce's belt loops.

"I'll allow the cuddles, just no kisses," Pierce told the warlock.

"Yes. Cuddles first, then my cock in your ass. It's a slippery slope, my wolf friend." I snorted out a *giggle*, and Alec interrupted me by pulling my chin up to him with his other hand. "Or maybe I'll take your ass instead. How would you like that, my lovely witch?" Pierce tensed against me, and Alec held his breath waiting for me to answer.

Honestly, the thought of being sandwiched between them like this and taking both of them at once had me intrigued. I lifted my head to give Alec a delicate kiss, and he responded with much more fervor than someone who was half asleep. His stubble scratched my chin, the sensation inflaming my skin all over. "If you want to fuck my ass, Pierce and Gilbert are welcome to as well. Fair is fair."

"Wonderful," Gilbert's voice said from above my head, and we all looked to see him hovering over us. He slowly raised his eyebrow at me, arousing me further. "I just need to work out how to fuck you at all before I fuck your ass. Though it's definitely a higher priority now."

I pointed a finger at him and narrowed my eyes. "Theseus."

"I, ahh..." The ghost pressed his lips together with a pleading look. "I didn't want you to be upset." Rolling onto my back, I crossed my arms over my chest and just let the silence indicate my mood.

"We're not going back to sleep, are we?" Alec complained in a whisper.

Giving Gilbert one final glare, I rolled over until I was on top of Alec, and I rested my head on his chest.

"When I wake up, there'd better be coffee."

8

OPENING UP

After falling asleep with my men surrounding me, I actually did wake up to the smell of coffee.

Do I have the best soulmates, or what?

Blinking, I opened my eyes to find that Gilbert was still hovering over the bed, watching me with a contented look on his transparent face.

Goddess, please tell me I didn't fart in my sleep.

Gilbert noticed the embarrassed look on my face and gave me a small smile. "You farted twice."

"*Mother fucker.*" My cheeks reddened and I heard someone in the kitchen.

"Gilbert, did you piss her off? Kinda the opposite of what we want, man." Pierce poked his head into the bedroom with a dish towel in his hands, and I sat up to get a better look at him. In the early morning light, he was looking mighty tasty. Ignoring how delicious he was, I squinted when I fully processed his choice of words, and Pierce gave me a disarming grin when he realized what I was thinking. "Always so suspicious."

I slid off the bed and walked to the dresser, running my hand over the brown surface as I opened a drawer. "With you three, it's kind of a necessity." I brought out some clothes to wear and took them with me to the bathroom, booping Pierce's nose as I passed him.

The kitchen had delectable smells coming from it, not all of which were coffee, but I ignored it for the moment so I could get dressed. I put on a purple crop top and a tight black skirt, one that would definitely show my ass if I bent over. After brushing my hair and putting on some lipstick, I emerged from the bathroom and was pleasantly assaulted with the smell of bacon.

"Hello, darling," Alec greeted from the stove, not looking up as he bent over a skillet. One of his hands shot out and he snapped to send a wave of magic that brought a coffee pot and mug to my chair. Already seated at the table, Pierce and Gilbert watched the coffee pot magically tip over and pour coffee into my cup. Mere seconds later, a cup of milk hopped over, along with a spoon full of sugar, and they emptied themselves into the mug too.

"Did you watch Beauty and the Beast last night or

something?" I commented as the pot, cup, and spoon trotted through the air to the counter where they stopped moving, and my mug of coffee gently placed itself in front of my spot at the table.

Alec spun from the stove with the skillet in his hands, and a plate flew up to him as he was scooping out pieces of bacon for me. "I guarantee if you were my prisoner in my castle, we'd skip the library and go straight to fucking. No polite shit for us." Another plate came flying up and Alec dished out some bacon for Pierce before a third plate emerged that he filled with the remaining pieces. "Eat up," he said as he sat down. "We've got a busy day ahead of us."

"Ahh, yes, blending in with the humans in the Ordinary city." I rolled my eyes and took a bite of bacon, crunching it between my teeth. "Please tell me that's not considered fun."

"We shall be doing no such thing, my dear." Alec paused to eat some of his food, passing the three of us a few slices of toast. His mouth was full when he spoke again. "Today we're taking you out."

"Out?"

"A date," Pierce clarified, taking my hand and giving it a kiss.

"Where we can all be together all day," Gilbert continued. "Pierce can be in his human form, and I can be there by your side. No hiding, and no chance of being caught."

I clutched a hand to my chest and felt it bursting with warmth as my excitement grew. That was exactly what I wanted, spending time with all three of my men. The only thing that would make it perfect would be Gilbert being a person again. A real, solid, living person. One that could hold my hand, wrap me in his arms at night, but if I didn't find his body and resurrect him, that would never happen.

We finished eating and I waited in the living room while the boys got their things and put their shoes on.

If this was my house, I'd want to decorate it. Coffins, and stars. Pumpkins, and skulls. Maybe even have a stupid bowl of potpourri, just because. I'd hang some spiderweb patterned curtains, put some spoopy[1] pillows on the couch. Find a dumb painting of a flower and hang it up right next to the door. And below it, four little hooks for our keys.

Could I plan for that life?

Nothing about our situation felt solid. We were one tremor away from it breaking.

"Love," Alec called to me, and I turned to see him standing by the door with Pierce and Gilbert beside him, and Alec's hand was stretched out for me to take. I came closer and took it, pressing our fingers together, and Alec clicked his tongue at my absent expression.

"You're here one second and gone the next. Where've you gone this time, my darling?"

I leaned into him and breathed in the smoky scent of his coat. I couldn't really vocalize what was bothering me, so I picked something else that was on my mind. "We've all slipped so easily into being together. It should've taken time, but I feel like we've been together all our lives." I slid a hand inside Alec's coat and gripped his shirt with my fingers. "It's only been two weeks since I was making Santa jokes and you kept trying to stare at my panties."

"To be fair," he breathed against my hair. "I'm still trying to stare at them."

Pierce handed me my sandals from the shoe rack. "Let's go, Jaz." I leaned against Alec to put my shoes on, and Pierce whisked me to his side when I was done. "Don't think about anything else today. Not school. Not the centaur. Not our families. Not anything. If I catch you thinking, I'm lifting that skirt up and spanking you."

I know I already said it, but, *bossy*.

"You keep up that talk and we won't be leaving this apartment," Alec said, and he thrust the door open before walking out to the hallway. "Pollyanna, Andi." I could hear our dorm mates outside talking to him. Pierce helped me put my backpack on, and he shifted into a wolf as Gilbert disappeared into the ceiling.

Pollyanna waved to me when I came out into the hall

and locked the door behind me. "Hey, Jaz! Are you excited about today?" She was wearing a bright yellow dress that matched the yellow and black plaid of Andi's pants. "Do you guys want to sit with us on the bus?"

"Sorry, lovely," Alec told her, and she started pouting. "We're not going with the school today. I'm taking Jaz on a date."

"Ohhh!" Pollyanna cooed, cutely popping her leg back with her hands pressed to her chin. "You guys are going to have so much fun!" Then she bent in front of wolf Pierce and clapped her hands against her knees. "Race you outside, doggie!" Pierce barreled after her when she took off running, and Andi followed behind them until we heard the front door opening.

I waited a few moments to make sure no one would overhear me, especially Pierce, and I came close to Alec, sliding my hands under his jacket and resting my head against his chest. "Alec, I love him."

He didn't ask me to clarify which of the other two I meant. He didn't say anything, he just put his warm arms around me and clutched me closer. "I know," he said, gently smoothing my hair away from my face.

"I've never told anyone I loved them before. Not Taylor, not anyone."

"Not everyone says I love you with words, Jaz. But it doesn't hurt to hear them." He tipped my chin up so I had to look into his steel eyes. "I know you're not ready to say it to us yet, and that's okay. Just remember that no matter what, no matter where our lives take us, we will never betray you. Your heart is the greatest treasure in all the realms. I would rather die than hurt you."

My chin wobbled under his gaze, and my chest burned with the same feeling that Pierce had given me. "I made up my mind to trust all of you with me, I've just had a little trouble doing it. If I lost any of you… My mom lost her soul mate. I wouldn't survive that, Alec."

He bent and pressed our foreheads together, thrumming my body to life with his hands stroking my sides. "I am not going anywhere, Jaz Neck. Even if I was dead, I would never leave your side." I took several deep breaths, trying to steel myself against my emotions. "Jaz, I told you this before. You can tell us anything."

"Us," I repeated with a small grin. "You always say us instead of me."

"I would never exclude Pierce or Gilbert from a statement like that." One of his hands quickly moved from my back to grasp one of my ass cheeks, making me gasp and push closer to him. "I'd love to be incredibly selfish and have you all to myself, but both of them are bastards and they would just steal you right back. Not that I don't enjoy the competition."

I felt his fingers slide onto the other side of my ass, and he squeezed with both hands until a hiss slipped out of my lips. "When we get back home, I'm sitting on

Santa's lap, and I'll tell you exactly what I want for Christmas."

"Mmmm," he mused, his mouth curling and smoke coming from his nose. "I'm not thrilled at you changing the subject, but that is definitely a diversion I can get behind."

Stepping back, I crooked a finger at him and led the way down the stairs and outside where Pollyanna was playing fetch with Pierce.

I stayed back, smiling when Andi waved to us. "Alec, there's something we need to do before we leave. The umm..." I gulped and remembered how he'd felt about what had happened at the dance. No matter that he seemed over it, I was still afraid of upsetting him.

"The centaur ghost, I know. Gilbert brought us up to speed."

"Okay, for real, do you guys have daily debriefs about me or something?"

He shrugged, which wasn't an answer, and put his hands in his pockets. "You're in luck that today is a field trip. Cauldron always opens up a large section of the barrier so we don't bottleneck at the doorway. The centaur can get out without our help, but we'll make sure he does."

After hearing the front door open, we turned to see two other couples coming out of the soulmate dorm. One was a boy and girl holding hands, the other was two boys, and both Pollyanna and Andi greeted them from the lawn. While everyone gathered to chat, Pierce ran up and barreled me over onto the grass, running his large tongue across my face.

Gross.

Alec chuckled behind his hand as I wiped at my cheek. "Alright, Pierce. Let her up."

As punishment for his slobber on me, I bounced up from the grass and mounted Pierce's sturdy back. "Giddy up," I said to him, and screamed when he took off running across the lawn. I grabbed at his fur and held on for dear life, because he didn't stop until we were at the barrier with all of the other students.

"Nice mount, Neck!" someone teased from the crowd.

Ignoring them, I slid off of Pierce's back and my knees wobbled until I knelt on the ground. Not my preferred method for getting wobbly legs.

"Damn it, Pierce," I whispered close to his ear, and he licked across my cheek again until I was smiling at him. I wished we could communicate when he was in this form. If only I was a telepath. That was a much cooler ability than moving stuff around with my mind.

Alec came running up to us and stopped next to me, skidding slightly in the dirt. He picked me up and wordlessly checked me all over, just in case I'd been injured. He always fussed over me. Grinning at him, I lifted my hand to brush some of his tousled hair out of his eyes, then he took my wrist to plant a kiss on my skin.

"Wotcher!" Gilbert shouted above my head, and thankfully no one else seemed to hear or notice him. The ghost of Theseus trotted up to hover beside Gilbert, nodding his head to me when he saw us.

"Creepy centaur ghost," Alec greeted. "The barrier should be open for you. We wish you... umm... a pleasant afterlife."

Gilbert pat the centaur on the shoulder. "Find a nice horse ghost and settle down."

Theseus shrugged him off and rolled his eyes. "It is no wonder you're both with the witch," he grumbled, lowering himself until he was close to me, his hair waving around his transparent chest. "Thank you for helping me." I was almost touched until his eyes traveled down to rest on my boobs.

Alec stiffened when he noticed, and smoke started coming from his nose. "Eyes front and center, pony."

Theseus half-neighed and shook his hair around. "Until we meet again, witch." And then he trotted above our heads, through the open barrier, and disappeared beyond where we could see.

Somehow, it eased the ache inside me, knowing his spirit was free. It didn't erase my failure over being unable to resurrect him, but I didn't feel quite as bad about it.

"Are you okay?" Alec asked, sliding his hand around my waist.

Gilbert lowered himself to stand in our circle, his tunic flapping around in the wind. I'd made a vow to find his body and resurrect him. If I had the powers to bring Gilbert back, I might be able to rectify Theseus' resurrection too. I couldn't do that if I never used my magic again, but I was still terrified at losing another life.

"Maybe," I answered slowly, and adjusted my backpack before tucking some of my long curls behind my ear. "I'll let you know."

The crowd around us started moving forward, but Alec held me closer and made me stay still. I wiggled around, only to be rewarded with him cracking his hand against my ass.

"You *cock*," I ground out, and he smirked at me which only served to piss me off further. He didn't let me go until everyone had gone down the hill to Highborn Village where the school buses awaited. Pierce sneezed and Gilbert shimmered as the light caught his body, but no one moved.

Before I could wonder why, in the distance I heard the sound of car locks being disarmed and an engine starting, the roar of it coming closer and closer to us until...

A vintage Cadillac rolled up the hill, coming to a stop in front of us with a puff of dirt that got in my mouth.

The body of the car was covered in nebulas and stars, all moving around like the night sky.

Alec took my arm, twisted it so my palm was facing up, and when he let my wrist go, there was a keychain sitting on my hand.

"What's this?"

"Keys."

I deadpanned him and almost threw the keys at his face. "Don't be such a jizz wizard."

Rolling his eyes, he gestured with his entire arm in the direction of the car. "Yours, mi'lady. I had someone from the estate staff bring it. It's my father's favorite car. He gave it to me last year for my birthday, but now it belongs to you."

I stared down at the keys and back up at the car, dumbfounded for a few moments, enough that Alec looked positively gleeful. "You... you're giving me a car?"

"Technically, soon everything I own will belong to you, but I wanted to give you this first. I thought it might make everything more real when the rest follows." He walked to the starry driver's door and opened it for me. "Your chariot awaits."

Fuck yes!

---

1. This is not a typo :D

9

THE ZOO DATE

"Darling," Alec said in a shaky voice from the passenger seat. "Perhaps, maybe, you should—*Jasmine!*"

Wildly spinning the wheel, I pulled the car into a spot and shifted into park. "I like making you shout my name, Alec." I raised an eyebrow at him as he tried desperately to catch his breath. "Jesus, *Driving Miss Daisy*. Have you never sped before?"

"*Not like that!*" he ground out, his messed-up hair starting to look like a rat's nest. Still trying to regain his dignified persona, he smoothed some of his curls down and straightened his jacket.

"That... was... *awesome!*" Pierce yelled from the backseat. He was safely buckled in, unlike Alec, and cutely wiggled his legs at me. "Again!"

Gilbert appeared on top of the car hood, looking winded despite his lack of functioning lungs. "Cauldron sparks! I fell off three blocks ago."

I unbuckled my seatbelt and got out of the car, stretching in the empty parking spot beside it as the boys joined me. With Alec still scowling at me, I fluffed some of his strewn hair around with a smile. "So, where's this date happening at?" I looked around the parking lot that Alec's directions had led us to, but it didn't seem extra special. It was across the street from some small-town boutiques and a deli restaurant, nothing too horribly interesting.

Alec goosed my ass and smirked when I jumped with a squeal. "We've got you for the entire day. The only thing you have to worry about is that no one from Highborn will see us." He took my right hand and Pierce took my left, then we started walking across the parking lot.

As we walked through the town, I marveled at how good it felt being out in the open with all three of them. I could hold Pierce's hand as long as I wanted, and every time I looked up, Gilbert was there. The cherry on top was having Alec by my side. It was magical. I didn't even care where we were going. We could've spent the day at a livestock auction, as long as it meant being with them.

I'd long since stopped paying attention to everything around me, as I was too busy alternating between leaning close to Pierce and reaching up to kiss Alec's cheek. Or sometimes kissing Pierce's cheek, and leaning close to Alec.

"What do you think?" Alec asked suddenly, and I realized we'd stopped walking. I looked up to see a sign above our heads that said we were at a zoo. My eyebrows raised in surprise, just before my face broke out in a grin.

"I *love* the zoo!" Pulling on their hands, I directed our group towards the ticket counter and cuddled against Pierce while Alec got us in line for our tickets. Gilbert stayed nearby and caught my eyes, making my stomach flutter. While he was waiting to pay, Alec took my arm and kissed my wrist as Pierce nuzzled my ear. Amidst the wave of desire I was feeling, I noticed some of the people staring at us and panicked.

"Alec," I whispered, squeezing his hand. "Alec, they're staring." I pulled Pierce closer to me and craned my head around the pavilion to make sure that in my distracted state I hadn't missed a magical beast or witch amongst the Ordinaries.

"Relax, darling." Alec kissed my forehead and rubbed at my shoulder until I relaxed slightly. "There's no one here to tattle on us. They're staring because we're poly. You know how Ordinaries can be about monogamy."

Ahh, right. That.

There were more than a few dirty looks directed at us, several that were in Pierce's direction specifically.

If anyone hurt my wolf, they'd regret it.

I wasn't going to let them spoil our date, especially since today was my first *real* day with Pierce, a day where no one had to hide. I could kiss him, hold him, do anything we wanted. Well, maybe not *anything*. Although, knowing Alec, if there was a quiet corner to fuck in, he'd find it.

My warlock grabbed me around the waist and we walked through the archway that separated the ticket counter and the gift shop, stopping at the bathrooms.

"So, where to first, my darling?" Alec asked brightly. As it was a cold November morning, not to mention a school day, the zoo wasn't horribly packed, giving us breathing room to explore. "And don't you dare think of wandering off or I'll have to tie us together," he added sternly.

I rolled my eyes and looked around, contemplating whether I wanted to veer left to the lions, or right to the monkeys, but something came over me, a weird feeling I couldn't explain. It was definitely magical, but I didn't know what was causing it. Maybe there was an animal corpse nearby? I tried to shake it off and chose the left path, bringing the boys to the lions so we could watch them lounging in their pen.

The male lion saw Pierce and stood to shake out his mane before roaring in challenge at the Lycan.

"That happen often?" Alec asked, and Pierce shrugged with a grin.

"I've been meaning to ask you," Gilbert started, setting down beside me. "What happened that turned your hair pink?"

"Turned? You mean that's natural?" Pierce asked as he grabbed a few of my curls to inspect the pink tips.

Alec watched the female lion pacing the pen, and a shadow crossed over his face. "When a witch has an unnatural hair color or tattoos, it's not something they did to themselves. It comes from pain. Emotional. Physical. Mental."

I looked at the grass by my shoes and slipped my fingers into my backpack straps. "The pink showed up when my dad died. At his funeral, I remember Abuela saying she was glad it wasn't my entire head because then I'd never find a boyfriend. Boys wouldn't want someone that damaged."

"Untrue," Alec said quietly. He brushed some of my hair off my shoulder and kissed the bare skin there. "I will gladly stay by your side, no matter how many tattoos you have, or how pink your hair is."

"Me too," Gilbert added. He came up behind me and pulled me into a hug, making me even colder, but I didn't care. My smile could've lit up the night sky when he kissed right behind my ear, and he felt so solid, so real.

Pierce put his hands on the outer cage bars, making the male lion roar again to warn him off. "You're beautiful no matter what, and your Abuela sounds like she sucks."

"You have no idea," I said under my breath. "We should probably move on before Mr. Lion decides to take a piece out of you."

Pierce purposefully avoided the predator animals, but the prey ones didn't like him much either, so he stayed at arm's length to let us enjoy everything because I refused to let go of his hand. It was clear the animals' reactions bothered him, but he was also used to it. I wondered if he'd ever had a pet, since it seemed like animals weren't comfortable around him.

Alec left for a minute, so we stopped at the grizzly bear enclosure to wait for him. The large animal was asleep on some rocks, letting me feel safe enough to pull Pierce closer until he stood beside me and I leaned my head on his shoulder. The bear's fur was waving with the wind, and it looked exactly like Pierce's fur, only brown instead of silvery white.

"Bet he's soft like you," I commented, squeezing Pierce's hand.

He snorted and slipped his arm around my waist. "Please. He's probably coarse and prickly. My fur is much better."

"I'll be the judge of that," Gilbert proclaimed, and he slipped through the enclosure gate with me grasping at the edge of his tunic.

"*You idiot!*" I shouted, but he kept going until he stopped next to the bear, watching it for a few seconds, and he bent to pet at its fur.

Pierce chuckled at the way I was bending to peer through the bars to make sure Gilbert was okay, and he pulled me closer to kiss my cheek. "You fuss over him like he's alive. Nothing can hurt him, Jaz."

"*Now*," I responded under my breath. "Nothing can hurt him *right now*. What will happen when I find his body and resurrect him? He can't take risks like that."

My ghost returned with a triumphant look on his face, completely oblivious to my scowl in his direction. "Pierce is softer."

"Yes!" my Lycan cheered, pumping his fist in the air, and the two high-fived above my head.

Boys.

Pierce kissed my cheek again. "Be right back, babe."

I watched him go down the sidewalk and leaned against the outer fence of the bear enclosure. Gilbert's chilly arms came around me, holding me close to him. From the Ordinaries' perspective, I was simply leaning against the fence. They had no idea I was in someone's cold but comforting embrace.

"I love you," he whispered in my ear, and rested his chin on my head. He hadn't said it for so long, and that suddenly upset me. I wanted to hear it more often. "You're an interesting soul, Jaz."

I threaded our fingers together on my waist. "I hope you mean interesting as in awesome, and not as in weird."

"Definitely awesome. You're just so used to dealing with everything on your own, you've always been so closed off. And now, with us, you're opening up, little by little. Part of me is mad because I'm not the sole cause of it, but I'm so happy to see you like this."

"Jealous boy," I retorted with a smile. With the cold November air and Gilbert's ghostly chill, I was starting to wish I had something hot to drink, but I wasn't about to let him move away from me. "I wish…" I stopped myself and lowered my head to stare at the rusty metal gate.

Gilbert didn't need me to say more, he already understood me so well, and he wordlessly wrapped himself more around me until my entire back was ice cold. "I know. I wish I was alive too."

No, tears! You will not be making an appearance!

Sniffing to hold the tears at bay, I straightened and stared up at the sky. "I don't even know how to *start* finding your body."

"Ouija board maybe?" We both giggled and he ran his hands through my hair, ghosting over the strands and drawing a shiver from me. "We'd probably need a high-powered tracking spell, something honed in to my specific aura. I'm not sure we can get that with witch magic. If we had some of my blood, a werewolf could find me." He contemplated it for a bit, and I was again struck with his knowledge of magic that was far beyond mine. But also, I never studied, so that wasn't hard to top. "The Fae, maybe. They deal with bone magic. If we could find one, they might be able to… help." He paused, for good reason, because the magical beasts wouldn't help us. They hated us, and if we went to the Unseelie court, they'd kill us where we stood. Pierce would have immunity, but once they heard what the spell was for, they'd probably execute him for being a traitor.

There was always…

I shook my head and rolled my eyes at my absurd thoughts, but it was the only option I could think of.

"There's always the necromancy cult."

"*WHAT?*" Gilbert shrieked in the true Gilbert fashion of overreacting, and more than a few of the nearby Ordinaries started mentioning how it had gotten colder all of the sudden. I turned to face him so my back wouldn't be covered in ice. "They *kidnapped you!*"

"I was there, I remember."

"Absolutely not," Gilbert pronounced, and I narrowed my eyes at him.

"Okay, fine, be like that. But let me know when you come up with a better option."

An uncomfortable silence fell between us, because he knew there wasn't a better option, he just wasn't willing to do it, and as much as I cared about him, it royally pissed me off.

He broke the stare-off and scrubbed a hand down his ghostly face. "You're right."

"I'm sorry, didn't catch that."

Giving me a flat look, he approached and pulled me against him, his ghostly semi-hard erection pressed against my stomach. "I will never compromise your safety for any reason."

It must've looked weird to anyone passing by when I reached my hand out and trailed it up Gilbert's tunic, right on top of that delicious cock of his. To anyone watching, I was patting at the air, and making the air hiss through their teeth when my fingers curled delicately around the air's penis.

"I want you to be tangible," I whispered huskily to Gilbert. "I want to grab you in the middle of the night and feel your skin under my fingers. At all hours of the day, I want you to hold me without fear of dropping me or suddenly not being there. And most importantly." I gently squeezed my fingers around his length, enjoying the way his mouth popped open as he moaned for me. "I want your dick inside me. I want you to fuck me whenever and wherever we want. I will do whatever it takes for that to happen."

Gilbert looked momentarily dumbfounded, and it passed when his hand snaked around my neck to firmly grip my hair, that shocked arousal shifting seamlessly to his sexy controlled stare. "Necromancer cult it is."

I tightened my hand around his cock and he pulled at my hair more until my heels lifted off the ground. "If you kiss me, it's going to look super weird to everyone nearby," I whispered breathlessly. He grinned devilishly at me, and I felt damp in all the right places. Okay, definitely didn't care who saw. Kiss me until I lose IQ points.

"I leave you two alone for five minutes and you're groping the air for all to see." Alec approached, holding a little cardboard drink holder with three Styrofoam cups inside it. Gilbert released my hair as Alec handed me one of the cups. The sides were hot to the touch, but I gratefully clutched it to my cold fingers and took a scorching sip anyway.

Fuck, that was some good coffee.

I gulped down more, and that weird feeling returned, coiling my stomach into a knot. Why was the zoo making me so uneasy?

Alec sipped at his coffee and set the holder down at our feet so he could put a warm arm around me. "You're freezing, darling. You should've worn a thicker coat."

Gilbert looked mournfully apologetic, as he had caused some of the chill inside me, but I didn't care. I'd cuddle him until I got frostbite. But still, I was definitely looking forward to the day when he'd be as warm as Alec and Pierce.

Alec kissed the top of my head. "What were you two discussing that required your hand on his cock? Plans for later? I'd love to watch, if that's the case."

"Finding my body," Gilbert answered simply, leaving out the important parts of the conversation.

"Ahh, so definitely making plans for later, then." Alec took another drink and rubbed at my shoulder, his proximity and the coffee already warming me up. "Any progress on that front?"

Before we could answer, Pierce returned and swept me in a hug. "I'm sorry I was gone for so long. God, you're freezing." He rubbed at my arms too and kissed my cold cheek, then Alec handed him the last cup of coffee.

"Come on, you'll warm up faster if we keep walking," Alec said. After throwing away the drink holder, he took my hand and led us through the zoo, past elephants and giraffes. We'd just finished our coffee when we passed by a bobcat that was the size of a regular cat, and I bent to look at him through the glass wall of his enclosure.

"Awwwwww—"

"*NO!*" Alec shouted, interrupting my cooing. "We are not bringing anything home. Absolutely not."

I lifted my hand and flipped him off over my shoulder. "I seem to recall you stealing something from a zoo, once upon a time. Something pink. Fluffy. Ring any bells?"

"I am a terrible example, and one that you should not follow." Snorting, I stood and felt wobbly as a rush of that weird feeling hit me, something tugging on me. I clutched a hand against my head to try and shake it off, making all three of my men hover over me. "Jaz, are you okay?"

"Do you need some water?"

"Are you still cold?"

Of course, my first reaction was telling them to stop fussing over me, but then I remembered what Gilbert had said. I'd always thought people fussing over me was unnecessary because I could take care of myself. Maybe that wasn't true.

The feeling was still there, but I ignored it enough to tip toe up to Alec's ear and whisper, "Where's the make out spot here?"

He was off faster than a cheetah, pulling Pierce and me along the sidewalk. Alec took us to an indoor exhibit, one that had several enclosures with cute bunnies and lizards. Even in the dimmed lighting, I could see some Ordinaries nearby, looking at the animals.

"Alec, I'm sure there's a better spot than this," I whispered.

He waited for a group of Ordinaries to pass, then he

snapped out some magic to a nearby door that said, '*Staff Only.*'

I hesitated briefly when he opened the door and tugged us all inside. As he closed it behind us, that weird feeling had gotten even stronger, to the point where it was getting harder to ignore. The lights in the bright hallway were way too bright for me to handle, and the animal smell made me nauseous. As soon as the feeling became unbearable, it died down again.

Blinking to clear my head, I noted several security cameras pointed where we were standing. "A... Alec," I whispered, and motioned to them.

"Never to worry, my dear," he answered confidently. "We're cloaked, they won't see us."

Pierce pulled some of his hair back into a ponytail. "I feel less guilty about the janitor's closet now."

"Just know that I'm taking notes on this sexy danger thing, and I intend to have my own spin on it," Gilbert informed us, crossing his transparent arms over his tunic.

I stepped backwards, going further down the hall, and gave them a mischievous smile. "You'll have your chance right now, if you can catch me."

I spun and took off running.

Now, admittedly, running from them wasn't a very smart plan. Alec and Gilbert could fly, and Pierce in both of his forms was formidable. I figured they would indulge me and let the chase go on for a bit, just to amp us all up, and I was right. Running as fast as my short self would allow, they still weren't catching up to me. I turned at a corner and side stepped the zoo workers that were standing in the hallway, the smell of animals getting more pronounced as I went.

Someone's fingers grabbed at the back of my blouse, prompting me to open the closest door, which turned out to be a laboratory. One of my pursuers got hold of me once I was inside, and we skidded across the floor, stopping at one of the metal tables.

It was Alec who had me, and he wasted no time lifting me up on to the table, planting himself between my legs, and scorching my lips with a fevered kiss.

Pierce was next, pulling me down to his lips and biting along my skin with a growl, his fingers shoving my skirt up so he could spread my legs more. And in a surprising twist, Gilbert was able to gently move him aside, and my ghostly lover kissed my breath away until every inch of my skin was enflamed and goosebumps popped out all over me from his chill.

When Gilbert's cold lips moved down to my neck, I heard noises in the small room and realized we weren't alone. Two Ordinary workers were in the laboratory, bent over something on another table, and they appeared to not have noticed us at all, even though we were making enough noise to raise the dead.

No pun intended.

With Gilbert on my neck, my lips were free for Alec to claim again, and Pierce's hands skirted across my thighs to where my panties were on clear display.

"It's a thrilling feeling, knowing that at any second we could be discovered," Alec breathed against my lips, his hand holding my neck in place beneath him. Pierce's fingers trailed over the front of my panties, right where a wet spot had formed from my arousal. "If they could see you right now, they'd see how *desperate* you are for us."

I was so overtaken with desire, I almost didn't notice the weird feeling taking over me in a sickening rush that did nothing to dampen my reaction to him. Alec was right, I was desperate for them. I needed them all over me, and I didn't care who saw. I would skirt danger every day for them.

Goddess, I think I love…

A squeak sounded in my ears, and it became the only noise that I could hear. Alec continued talking to me, saying something I'm sure was very sexy and highly inappropriate, I just didn't hear it. There were more squeaks, some scurrying around on a piece of paper. My eyes darted around the room to see what was making that noise when one of the Ordinaries moved, and it happened.

I saw my familiar.

Staring at the little gerbil cage it sat in, my eyebrows

knit together in confusion. What was it? It looked like a little ball of brown fluff with two enormous eyes. It was also tiny, about the size of my palm. Still, what was it, I had to ask again.

I sad.

A small, frail voice was in my head, and I barely noticed that Alec's stance had changed to concern and Pierce's hands left my crotch. They helped me off the table as I tried to step down, that little creature overtaking my entire focus. Alec gripped my arm and seemed to understand what was happening, though I still couldn't hear him.

Mommy?

Okay, what? I was no one's mommy, especially not a fluff ball.

A pouting emotion sat in my head, the creature wordlessly expressing displeasure with me. Great. I'd had a familiar for five seconds and it was mad at me.

Want out.

Both of the Ordinaries turned, and one picked up the little cage, heading towards the door we'd entered through.

No! They couldn't take him away from me. He was *mine*. My powers started to rumble inside me, and various objects in the room lifted in the air.

"Behold!" I just barely heard Alec say before smoke unfurled from his nostrils and filled the room. As my hearing was still mostly gone, I was also blinded by the smoke, and those fucking Ordinaries were making off with my *baby*— oh my god, what is happening right now.

Through the smoke, I felt a hand taking mine, Pierce's judging by the roughness of his skin, and it led me out of the room, through a smoke filled hallway, and out a door that beeped loudly when we opened it. I snapped my fingers to shut off the annoying beeping, and the smoke cleared to show Alec standing nearby, without the gerbil cage.

I better not have done all that for a fucking *gerbil*.

I had to trust he'd retrieved the animal, even though I really wanted to check to be sure. He motioned for us to follow him away from the building, which was a good idea considering we'd just stolen *whatever it was* from the zoo, and they'd be searching for it, and us. We followed close behind Alec until we were a block away from the zoo entrance.

Before Alec stopped walking, I tugged on his jacket sleeve and searched him for my familiar like I was looking for a hidden stash of cookies. "*Alec*," I shouted in frustration after his first few pockets turned up nothing. "Where is he? *Give him to me!*"

"What just happened?" Pierce asked, tugging me away from Alec, but I refused to stop rooting through his pockets, even though I could barely reach them.

Gilbert answered just as Alec put a hand to my forehead to hold me off. "She found her familiar."

Alec rolled his eyes as I clawed at him. "Calm down, Jaz, *goddess*, you're persistent. I have him, please stop that." I whined and he grabbed my hand to hold it out, then something warm and fluffy was on my palm, and Alec stepped back to give me space to examine what we'd just stolen.

"The *fuck*... is that?" Pierce's sentiments matched mine, because it looked like a fucking Furby. A little orangey-brown Furby.

Mommy...

"Okay, buddy," I addressed. "I am not your mommy."

Alec bent to stare at it, twisting his head this way and that. "What's he saying to you?"

"Not much. I'm not sure he really knows how to speak."

Gilbert reached a transparent finger out to its head and the little thing shied away. "He'll get better at it with time. Once you give him a name, we'll be able to hear him too."

"Ahh..." I stared down at the... for fuck's sake, what *was it*? "Furby would be a bit on the nose, right?"

"How about Merlin?" Gilbert suggested innocently, but the coincidence of his name choice and Gilbert's entire situation had me narrowing my eyes.

"I. Swear. To. God. If your past self was the great

wizard Merlin, I will drop kick you." When the name came from my lips, the little thing's tiny ears perked up. "You like it?" He squeaked at me in approval. "Mkay, welcome to the fam, Merlin."

UwU, Merlin said telepathically to all of us.

"Still not really sure what you are, little guy," I said to him, holding him closer to my face. "Might have to google it."

"Jaz! Hey! We weren't expecting to see you here— *oh my god*!"

We turned to see Taylor and Aurora approaching down the sidewalk, and with all four of us in clear view, there would be no chance to hide.

"*Fuck me*," I shouted, and stood in front of Pierce, stupidly trying to conceal him, but it was no use. They'd seen him, it was very obvious by the looks on their faces. Merlin scurried up my arm and hid inside my bra, his little warm body snuggled against my cold skin.

"We can explain," Alec began before anyone had said anything. Taylor was too busy gaping to speak, but Aurora looked like she had plenty of things to say.

"Jaz," she started. "I'd be very interested to know why this Lycan is here with you?"

"Again, we can explain," Alec tried again, but she silenced him with a glare.

"I wasn't asking you, Alec."

"There's definitely no need to be rude," Gilbert chastised, and Taylor's mouth popped open when he fully noticed who, or I should say *what*, was hovering beside me.

"Okay, where did this ghost come from?"

I reached behind me and gripped Pierce's hand. "We should probably..."

Aurora nodded. "We definitely should. There's a restaurant across the street. Let's go talk."

10

MY JEALOUS BOYS

The awkward silence at our table was thicker than Alec's ego.

Our waitress had already taken our orders and left to bring our drinks, though she did raise an eyebrow when we brought a sixth chair to the table for Gilbert to sit in. I put my bag in the seat to at least make it look like we were saving it for someone, and it sat in the middle of Gilbert's waist.

While Taylor was enamored with the fact that a ghost was sitting with us, Aurora's focus was solely on Pierce, and I couldn't tell if she was horrified or curious. "So..." She tapped one of her perfect nails against her deep brown skin. "Is this boy the wolf we saw at Highborn?"

"Pierce," the wolf in question said simply.

"Pierce, my apologies. But you are the wolf, yes?" He nodded to her. "Thought so, you smell the same."

"Aurora has my specialty too," Taylor explained. "Elemental with a focus on animals." He waited a few seconds, thrumming his fingers on the table and trying not to openly stare at Gilbert. "Where'd the ghost come from?"

His sister flicked him with her finger. "Not the important part, Taylor. They've been consorting with a Lycan."

"Jaz doesn't do anything without a reason, Aurora. I know she has one." Taylor searched my face and tried to relax his hands. "You do, right?"

With Aurora still trying to pin me with her stare, I looked down at the table and noticed a few crumbs on it. "Pierce is my soulmate. All three of them are." I quickly peeked at her and her eyebrows were raised all the way to her hairline.

"You're joking," she said with a half-laugh.

Taylor's mouth pressed to a thin line and he held his hand out to Pierce. "May I?" While they clasped hands, Pierce's fingers slid over my knee to keep me calm. "Hmm."

"Hmm?" Aurora echoed in question. "Hmm what?"

"I've never tried this with a Lycan before, but there's a bit of information here. They're telling the truth, Aurora. She's his mate." He let Pierce's hand go and put his own in front of him on the table. "Have you told Cauldron yet?"

Alec picked up a sugar packet from the little dish holding them and shook it like it owed him money. "No one at Highborn knows."

Aurora snorted and leaned back in her chair. "You guys are crazy to think Cauldron doesn't know. He's the most powerful wizard there is, apart from Jaz here. There's no way a glamour spell would fool him."

I hoped she wasn't right. But then again, if he *had* known this whole time, he'd never said anything.

Our waitress returned and distributed our drinks, setting my large cup of coffee in front of me, and I burned my already burnt tongue taking a large sip of it.

"Does anyone have any vodka? I prefer my coffee with vodka." Merlin wiggled around in my bra, his tail tickling me and making me squeal. "Be still, fluff ball!"

Taylor's face lit up like it was Christmas morning. "Do you have a pet with you? What is it? Can I see it?"

I hesitated to let anyone touch my little baby. I now understood why I rarely saw Alec's pink fairy armadillo, and I wondered how he had tolerated me holding her. My eyes darted to my Alec, and he gave me a nod of understanding, gesturing that I could bring Merlin out.

In full view of the restaurant, I reached into my bra and pulled out my little familiar, resting him on my palm for all to see. Taylor cooed excitedly and carefully put his hands near mine for Merlin to jump into. I expected the little creature to hesitate as he'd done when Gilbert tried to pet him, but instead, he happily hopped over to Taylor without hesitation. It had to be Taylor's specialty that made Merlin trust him, but I definitely didn't like someone else touching my familiar, even if Merlin didn't care. I squeezed Pierce's hand and tried not to bend closer to Taylor as he carefully inspected Merlin.

"Where'd you find him?" he asked in wonderment.

"Found him in the forest," Alec answered smoothly.

Aurora poked her finger in his direction. "Alec, you're shit at lying, and this is not a conversation you want to lie at."

"We stole him from the zoo," Pierce cut in before she could bite Alec's head off. "Wasn't really an option not to, just like Jaz and I."

Taylor gasped and lowered Merlin so he could scowl at me. "*Jasmine*! You can't go stealing animals from a zoo!" I shrugged and gulped more coffee, carefully watching Merlin over the rim. "He's a pygmy Tarsier, I think. Aurora?"

The pop star took Merlin, making me squeeze Pierce's hand harder, and she smiled as she pet at Merlin's head. "Definitely, that's what he is. Extremely rare, too. I'd say give him back, but I know that's not an option."

"No, it's not," Pierce declared, standing up and

retrieving Merlin from her, then he sat down and gave my baby back to me. My entire body relaxed, and I snuggled him against my cheek. "We need to know right now what's going to happen next. Are you going to turn us in?"

"I'd say there's no need to be so direct, but I'm afraid there is," Alec responded.

"And if we say we're turning you in?" Aurora asked him, making my chest squeeze.

"Then we'll go to the magical beasts and hope they're more forgiving than our own kind. And if they're not, then, maybe the vampires will let us in. Everyone knows they're off-limits, so I doubt either side of the war would go looking for us there, especially since the Lycans *might* take our side." Alec's answer was specific enough that I knew he'd already contemplated this, and judging by Pierce's lack of reaction, he had as well.

"Seems like you've got it figured out," Aurora noted dryly, her expression still not telling me which way she was leaning.

Alec's lips pressed together. "I will do whatever I have to in order to keep Jaz safe."

She started laughing, and that was more horrifying than any reaction I'd been picturing. "Oh, god, Taylor. I can't hold it in." Taylor started smirking and put a hand over his mouth to cover it. "I'm sorry, I'm sorry. I know I'm probably freaking you out right now."

"What the hell, Aurora!" Alec ground out as we watched them giggle to each other.

She got control enough to stop snorting and wiped at her eyes. "We're peace sympathizers."

"*What?*" I shrieked, making Merlin scurry back into my bra. "You were baiting us?" Taylor nodded with another laugh and we all deflated into our chairs. "*Fuck*, you little bitch. We were terrified!"

"I'm sorry, I'm really sorry, Jaz," he told me, trying to stifle a giggle. "It's not something we can just *tell people*. We had to be sure of your motives about Pierce being with you."

"*What did you think we were going to tell you, you cock!*" I threw sugar packets at them and they just laughed more.

"Fair," Aurora admitted with a smile. "But it's still better to be sure. And again, we're sorry."

Taylor threw some of the packets back at me and Pierce deflected them before they could hit me. "Now you're one of us."

Huh. I guess we were.

Our waitress returned with food, and unintentionally stuck her ass through Gilbert when she bent to slide me my plate of pancakes.

You better back that ass up, lady.

Once we all had our food and the waitress was gone, Taylor pointed his fork at Alec and Pierce. "So, tell me how you guys met Jaz."

Alec smirked, taking a bite of his steak. "Still in love with her, I see. I don't blame you, Jaz is an amazing woman." I wasn't close enough to kick him in the dick, but I gave him a glare that made it clear I wanted to. "We met when she returned to Highborn after specializing. Candace attempted to bully her, and Jaz sent her packing. Definitely caused a man-reaction, if you know what I mean, Taylor."

"Ugh, gross," Aurora complained, sticking her tongue out. "Don't make me picture that."

"Then," Alec continued around another piece of meat. "She pushed me off the stairwell. She didn't know I can fly, so you can imagine the look on her face when I *wasn't* lying dead on the bottom floor."

"I wasn't trying to kill you, you *ass*," I mumbled under my breath.

"Then we met at a pub and I kissed her, revealing that we're soulmates. Best day of my life."

Taylor went quiet, so Aurora stepped in. "How about you, Pierce?"

He devoured a fork full of burrito and put his arm over the back of my chair. "My pack was running through the forest outside of Highborn, and she and Gilbert were there. It only took one look, and I knew she was mine. Granted, I spent the next few hours having a crisis over it, but when we finally officially met, she didn't toss me out. She let me stay. She even let me kiss her." I smiled to myself and felt my cheeks flush.

Gilbert spoke up then, even though they hadn't gotten to him yet. "I met Jaz when she was fifteen. I just kind of... I don't know, appeared? And she was right in front of me, crying her heart out. I felt an overwhelming need to protect her, to stay by her side. I knew she was my soulmate without kissing her, but it was definitely confirmed when we kissed a few weeks ago."

The more they talked about kissing me, the more Taylor seemed to frown, and Aurora went quiet when she noticed. We slipped into an awkward silence again as we ate, the only sound coming from our silverware and Merlin's little snores.

When Aurora finished her food, she stood up and caught my attention. "Jaz, let's go to the ladies' room."

Oh, right, that thing girls did. I'd been without a close friend for so long, I'd forgotten about that little ritual, but I still stood and followed her away from our table, motioning to all of my men that they'd better behave.

After walking through the restaurant to where the signs led us, Aurora held the door open for me and we entered the girl's room. She went straight to the mirror, pulling out a tube of lipstick from her pocket and applied some on her lush full lips. Her lips made mine look flat, and I was very jealous of them.

She met my eyes in the mirror and smiled, her white teeth stark next to her dark skin. "I don't know if you noticed, but my brother is *so* jealous right now. The fact that his first girlfriend is not only off the market, but off the market with *soulmates*. There's no chance of stealing you back now."

It hadn't occurred to me that he'd *want* to, considering why we'd broken up.

"I'm sorry if I'm making you uncomfortable," she said softly.

I shook my head and pressed myself against the sink counter. "No, it's fine. I'm a little unused to interacting with people. Things didn't go very well for me after Taylor left. I've been mostly alone since then."

"Until you met those fine ass boys," she said with a half-groan of delight. "God *damn*, I think I'm more jealous than Taylor is. The *ass* on that wolf, I had to force myself to not stare at it so you wouldn't hit me. Normally I'm not into shorter men, but I would definitely not even care with him involved."

"Mkay, chill out, Aurora."

She laughed and put her lipstick back into her pocket. "That ghost isn't bad either. I assume you're going to bring him back?"

I chewed on my lip, fluffing my hair up a bit. "We have to find his body first. And I'm not... skilled enough yet."

She nodded and leaned her hip against the counter. "We heard the gossip at Highborn, about what happened with the centaurs. I'm sure my advice won't help, but you'll get there."

"So everyone keeps saying," I mumbled, knowing it was true, but I still felt like shit about my powers.

Mommy no sad, Merlin told me quietly.

"I do have to say," she said brightly. "You're the first witch that hasn't fangirled over me. Usually they're asking for my autograph left and right."

"I wish I could say it's because you're Taylor's sister, but in reality, I don't listen to your music unless it's playing at the Curse N' Save."

She laughed and gave me a playful shove. "I like you, Jaz. Ignoring how my brother would feel about it, I'd like it if we became friends. I could use one, and I'm sure you could too, not that I'm presuming." I'd barely nodded when she lunged forward to grab my shoulders. "Yay! I'm so excited. I hope you're fine with me texting you a lot. Where's your phone, we should sync up."

I produced my cell phone and she brought hers out, bumping them together to activate the spell all witch phones had, one that copied our numbers and sent it to the other person, along with a picture of the phone's owner.

That done, she checked herself in the mirror one last

time and washed her hands. "Let's go back before a fight breaks out over you."

Ha.

The table was definitely more tense when we returned, and it dissipated once my men caught sight of me. Everyone was finished eating, so we left the restaurant and went outside to the porch. I shivered in the cold wind and Alec and Pierce both started removing their coats for me. Pierce got his off first, triumphantly putting it over my shoulders with a smug grin.

Where was this coat when I was cold at the zoo? Show offs.

Aurora and Taylor walked with us back to my car, and while Pierce and Gilbert got into the back seat, Taylor pulled me aside until we were far enough away that my men wouldn't hear us.

"I'm happy for you, Jaz. Those are some good men you've got. I won't say I'm not jealous, because I am." He looked away, his smile not quite hiding the pain in his eyes. "You don't know how much I wished I was your soulmate. I would've given anything, but you didn't love me."

My heart twisted to see the look on his face. "Taylor, that's not fair. I cared about you."

"That's not love, sweetheart. And because you didn't love me, you didn't let me in. But them..." He pointed behind us to the car where Alec stood beside it, and

Gilbert and Pierce were checking on me through the side window. "They deserve all of you."

"I..." I swallowed and sighed, hating how Taylor always saw through me. "I know."

Being very brazen considering our audience, he carefully leaned over me for a comforting hug. "If those boys hurt you, they'll have me to deal with," he whispered in my ear, and I rolled my eyes with a snort.

"As if they wouldn't have me to deal with first. Also, you'd better end this hug quick, they hate other boys touching me." He chuckled and let me go, just before Alec came up and grabbed me to his side, only proving my point.

Aurora joined us, hiding a smile over Alec's jealousy. "Well, we have to run. We hope to see you guys again soon." She hugged me, and they started walking back towards the city.

Alec grumbled something under his breath while he walked me to the car, directing me to the passenger side so he could drive. The car was silent as he started it up and let it idle.

Sighing, I rolled my eyes and buckled my seatbelt. "He hugged me, you all saw it. Let's move past it."

"Absolutely," Alec responded, surprising me with how pleasant he seemed about it. Skeptical, I narrowed my eyes and studied him carefully. "Taylor is no threat, even if I want to thrash him for touching you."

"I still kind of do," Gilbert piped in from the backseat. "But you're right, no threat."

Why were they being so cool about it?

"It's because of how you looked at him," Pierce explained coolly, also completely fine with everything. "You don't look at us like that. I'm content."

I groaned in complaint, because they'd traded jealous fits for smugness. *I was going to punish the fuck out of them*, and I knew just how to do it.

11

JAZ'S SPECIAL NIGHTGOWN

We made it back to Highborn without incident, and I stayed silent while we went up to our room. Alec opened the door for us, carefully locking it so Pierce could shift back, and we all took our shoes off.

"I'm going to change. Meet me in the bedroom." They didn't comment, just watched me walk to the bathroom and close the door.

I loved how protective they were, I really did. That didn't mean I was going to let it slide with them being jealous about every single person that touched me. If it was because of me holding back, then I needed to be vulnerable and show them all of me, until they were absolutely certain that my affections were with them.

Resolute with my plans, I placed my coffin bag on

top of the counter. Unzipping it, I brought out several items and placed them around the sink. I shaved my legs and armpits with a magical razor, and briefly considered showering, but I'd need it more after what I was planning.

Removing all of my clothes, I placed a sleeping Merlin in a little nest I made from my shirt. It would definitely bother me with him not being close, but I knew exactly where he was, and if something happened, I'd be able to summon him to me.

With him safe, I put on the nightgown I'd brought out, slipped on a silky robe over it, then I brushed my hair. For a final touch, I applied some enchanted lipstick that wouldn't rub off.

Goddess, it's show time.

Once I opened the bathroom door, it would be impossible to get my soulmates to focus, so I hoped they were all in the bedroom like I asked. I zipped up my backpack and left it by the sink, then I turned the door handle and stepped out into the hallway, turning towards the bedroom. Without looking up at them, I leaned against the doorway and put my hands on the belt of my robe.

"So," I started.

All three of them made a noise that was somewhere between '*fuck me*' and like someone had just throat punched them.

"My jealous boys. Do you remember me telling you about my enchanted nightgown?"

More half words and squeaks.

"What you're feeling right now is only the partial effect with my robe covering it." I lifted my eyes and examined their reactions under the curtain of my lashes. Standing in various parts of the bedroom, they were basically drooling at me, which is exactly what I wanted. "Would you like me to remove my robe?"

"I might die," Alec began hoarsely.

Pierce finished his broken sentence. "But please do, for the love of god."

"*I'm about to ectoplasm my fucking pants.*"

Slowly, as I met each of their gazes, I undid my belt and slipped the robe off to pool on the floor around me. My nightgown was black sheer fabric that ended right at the apex of my thighs, which would've been covered by underwear, if I was wearing any, that is. The bodice was low cut, and the sheer fabric over my nipples left little to the imagination.

"I would like you three to know that I've never shown this nightgown to anyone before. It was a gift I bought myself last year, in the hopes that one day I'd have someone to wear it for. And now I do."

"Lucky us," Gilbert whispered, his mouth dropped open. The other two had the same look, and I was a little worried they would actually start drooling.

"Why can't I move to you? I feel like I'm frozen."

"Part of the spell woven into this nightgown renders anyone effected by it immobile, just in case there's someone watching that you'd rather not touch you. Only I can unfreeze you." I briefly enjoyed their gaping, and went to sit on the front of the bed, spreading my legs just enough where they could definitely see that I wasn't wearing anything underneath. "I also want you to understand that while I know I can't stop you from being jealous, that I can and will torture you over it."

"Cruel woman," Alec complained.

"Hmm," I mused, trying hard not to grin from ear to ear, and I inspected my nails, spreading my legs wider. "I should wear this during a school day under my clothes, and cast a personal space bubble so you're just driven wild but unable to touch me."

"I will never be jealous again, please have mercy," Pierce whined, and I did feel a little bad. A smidge.

Alec grunted at me, and it sent a shiver up my spine. "Alright, point taken. Please unfreeze me, I need to touch your tits. *God*, you are so gorgeous."

Standing, I slipped one of the straps off, baring my shoulder to them, and I could definitely see some drool on their faces now. "There is one thing you three should keep in mind the next time someone touches me." I pulled my arm out of the strap and the nightgown fell slightly to reveal one of my breasts. "*They're not you.*" The other strap was next, until the nightgown fell off me and pooled at my feet, leaving me flush and fully naked. I sat back down in the few seconds it took for the nightgown's effects to wear off, and my heart sped off as I waited for them to move.

They stayed still, long after I'd have expected them to be freed. Before I could start wondering if the nightgown's effects were much more powerful than I'd been told, Alec slowly closed the distance between us, staring down at me with the same heat he'd had when I was still wearing it.

"I'm very aroused right now, and I'm afraid I'm going to hurt you if I touch you," he said in a low voice. "But, by god, I can't stop myself."

He maintained eye contact with me as he removed his jacket and shirt, revealing his lean but toned body. When he unbuckled his belt, Pierce had figured out how to move again as well, and he tossed his shirt aside before almost tripping on his pants as he tried to walk and remove them at the same time. Gilbert already had his tunic off and was working on his trousers at the same time that Alec's pants fell to the carpet. I hadn't seen Gilbert naked before, but Alec interrupted my perusal of him by slipping the nightgown back over my head, and he made sure to leave one breast exposed, clearly enjoying how it had looked.

"I don't need this on, you know."

Alec hid a sheepish look with his practiced smirk. "Oh, I'm not putting it on for you. I have a feeling it's enchanted to make sure we last longer, and I'm going to climax instantly without it. That is a humiliation I'd rather not have."

"Same," Pierce and Gilbert admitted in the same breath, the gaping and drooling making a reappearance as the nightgown's effects returned.

They were all naked now, a buffet of delectable bodies and mouth-watering cocks, just waiting for me to unfreeze them. I reached my leg out and pressed a toe to Alec's chest, doing the same to Pierce and Gilbert, and once freed, they all lunged at me at once. Alec skidded me across the comforter until we were in the middle of the bed, kissing me like he was trying to devour my lips, the musky smoky scent of him driving me to a fever pitch.

Our lips parted, and I stared up into the cold steel of his eyes, every fear and insecurity falling away until I was only desire. Only love.

Alec dipped to kiss my neck, moving down my chest and planting kisses down the front of my nightgown, heading straight for the heat between my legs. Pierce and Gilbert were quick to take his spot on my upper half, with my Lycan kissing and nibbling along my neck, and Gilbert blowing puffs of cold air on my nipple until it stood at attention.

When Alec parted my thighs and did the same thing to my swollen clitoris, I gasped and arched my back against the mattress, almost making Pierce slide off me. He planted himself on my chest to keep me still, drinking in every moan and gasp I gave as he watched my face. Alec flicked my nub with his tongue, going slowly at first, then speeding up until I started thrashing and sinking my fists into the sheets. I was too wound up, too aroused. I wouldn't last very long, and I knew it.

My warlock knew it too, judging by the way he locked me in place with his arms around my hips, and sucked my clit in-between his lips. I moaned and gasped, hazily looking up at Pierce, and he was giving me that look that always made my stomach flutter. It was equal parts wild desire and a reminder that I belonged to him.

He tipped my chin up with his finger and watched my eyes roll back into my head as Alec's tongue was quickly bringing me close to the edge. "Eyes open," Pierce told me, and I did so, only so I could glare at him for being bossy again, but he picked the perfect moment because Alec's tongue lashing was starting to make my toes curl.

With him lapping at me like I was a fucking bowl of water, I threw my head to the side, practically ripped at my fistful of sheet, and my pleasure rose higher and higher. Pierce bit at my neck and kissed the stings away, the pain not even registering with my body so close to climax. I released one fist from the sheets and brought it up to Gilbert's neck, running my fingers through his cold hair, and I guided him to my lips mere moments before everything came down.

Gilbert's mouth seared mine with heat despite the chilly feel of his lips, and he didn't let me pull away when my legs lifted on their own, Alec's tongue flicked my clit one last time, and I started coming. My ghost kissed me through every wave, drinking in my moans until I went limp against the mattress.

It took me several minutes for my chest to stop heaving, and I felt deliciously drowsy. I didn't for one second think that they'd let me fall asleep, because they weren't done with me.

Once my body had calmed down, I opened my eyes to see all three men staring down at me, and Pierce helped me sit up so he could hold me close to him.

"Alec, sit at the headboard," he said, his eyes completely focused on my lips. Alec crawled behind me as Pierce claimed my lips, his rough and commanding kiss making my body thrum to life. Rather than ordering me again, which he knew I wouldn't obey, Pierce guided me on my hands and knees towards the headboard. Now I could clearly see Alec sitting at the front of the bed with his cock at full attention, and damn, it was making my mouth water. The barest hint of smoke came from his nose, and he watched Pierce gently pushing me forward until I was crawling up Alec's legs and we were face to face.

Pulling the nightgown up over my ass, Pierce used his knees to spread my legs wide, and then Alec got to stare into my eyes and see my reaction as Pierce slowly slid his rather large cock inside me.

Let me just say that Alec ate it up like Christmas cookies.

I had to flutter my eyes closed with my walls being deliciously stretched, my mouth popping open with a loud gasp, and Alec slipped his finger between my lips, anchoring it on my teeth.

"Pay close attention, Gilbert," Pierce said, his fingers sinking into my hips. "You'll see exactly how she likes it." He withdrew and thrust into me, making my arms wobble slightly, and then he started fucking me hard, each thrust going deep inside me at a steady pace. It wasn't as fast as I usually liked, but even so, it felt *so good* to have him inside me again.

Alec began gathering up my curls in one of his hands, enjoying the way I shuddered with Pierce slamming into me. Then he gave me one deep kiss and lowered my head to where his dick lay against his stomach. It was exquisitely mouthwatering with a small bead of moisture on the tip that I was definitely going to lick off. He helped guide my mouth to it as my hands were occupied with holding me upright, and Alec moaned long and low when I ran my tongue up the tip of his cock. That salty taste of him had me closing my lips around his head to get more of it, making him hiss and tug at my hair.

Something cold fluttered over my clit, and I gasped against Alec's cock, prompting him to gently slide it between my lips. Gilbert's fingers were definitely on my nub, and it was such a stark contrast to the heat there that it made my head spin. Pierce picked up speed from the sight of me sucking Alec's dick, I assumed at least, fucking me so hard and fast, I was in heaven.

Alec let me up for air, letting me trail my tongue around the tip again before his cock went back in. After giving me a few seconds to adjust, he started gently thrusting into my mouth. I'd never been fucked from both ends before, and I had to say, I was hella into it.

With my mouth full of dick, cold fingers sliding along my clit, and my pussy being pounded, a climax wasn't far off. I was straining for it, feeling it coming but not quite there. I clenched the sheets again to help ease my tension, thankfully having a welcome distraction by Alec's moans getting louder. While his thrusts were controlled and gentle, his grip on my hair was anything but, and he kept me there as he threw his head back and started shooting his salty come into my mouth.

His hand on my hair relaxed with him boneless against the headboard, and I lifted my head until his cock slipped from my lips. He opened his eyes just enough to see me visibly swallow.

"*Fuck*," he whispered in response. My head drooped with the reality of my impending climax coming back to me, and Alec grabbed my hair again, pulling me up to his face. "Make her come, Pierce." He drank me up, his chest still heaving from his orgasm, and when I felt that moment hit me, when I knew this was the final wave and I was about to come, smoke trickled out of his nostrils, curling around me like a caress.

My body tensed up and I could barely breathe. How was I still upright? I felt boneless and frozen all at once. Pierce's fingers dug into me, and he impossibly went faster, harder, *god* he knew how to fuck, he was pulling my orgasm from me like a rabbit from a hat.

Gilbert's fingers on my clit were almost too much. I inhaled sharply and let out a string of half-words until I shouted, "*Fuck!*" right as my body tipped over and I was coming, shuddering and clenching as I continued shouting '*fuck*' over and over. Pierce thrust into me until he too was shouting and slamming his come inside me. He let me go and pulled out, and I collapsed on Alec's lap, my limbs turned to jelly.

It took me several minutes to remember how to breathe properly, and when I surfaced, I was sandwiched between my warlock and Lycan, with Gilbert hovering over us. As I hazily looked up at him, he slowly grinned at me, a grin that promised a deep mind-altering fuck in our future. One that I was very much so looking forward to.

Alec had his arms around my waist, and Pierce's hands were rubbing at the spots on my hips that he'd been grabbing onto. "I'm not finished watching you come, my dear," Alec whispered in my ear. He paused, leaning in to kiss my bruised lips. "Do you remember that chat about fucking your ass?" My eyes widened and he lifted a hand, sending out magic to bring something to him, and a bottle appeared that he clutched with his fingers. It was definitely an anal sex potion, no doubt about that. The potion meant I'd feel no pain, need no prep or lube, and I would recover quickly afterwards.

"Where did you get that?"

He shrugged. "I always have some on me." I took it from him and uncorked it, then tipped it to my mouth and swallowed the grape flavored liquid while keeping eye contact with him. More smoke came from his nose as he watched, something I was beginning to tell was his version of a magical erection. Then he took the empty bottle and flung it across the room before roughly kissing me. "Up," he ordered, and he tugged Pierce up as well until we were all sitting on our knees.

It felt so natural being between them, my skin tingled at the feeling of Alec's chest against mine, and Pierce's against my back. Alec lifted me over his lap, and

I stared over his shoulder at Gilbert, moaning aloud when Alec slipped his cock inside my pussy.

My magic instantly reacted, flying out of me and covering us in its blanket. Alec's burst from him, holding mine down and making me moan against his shoulder. The extra sensations were going to drive me insane, but I wouldn't have had it any other way.

With one hand holding me against him, Alec's other arm went past me to Pierce, and the Lycan came closer until his cock bumped my ass. I could feel him hesitating, but Alec was right there.

"You can't hurt her, the potion makes sure of it," Alec assured him, kissing my shoulder to steady me.

I felt their clasped hands on my hip, and Alec pulled his away until it was only Pierce gripping me. My Lycan's hand traveled up my side underneath the nightgown and across to my stomach. He used it to steady himself before he carefully pushed inside my ass. I mentioned Pierce's cock was big, well, it felt much bigger in my backdoor than it did the front. I almost bit into Alec's shoulder trying not to moan loudly in case Pierce thought it was from pain. It definitely wasn't. The feeling was different, but also the furthest thing from unpleasant.

Pierce stopped halfway in and kissed at my back. "You okay?"

I nodded and didn't hide my next groan. *"Fuck me."*

They both took the hint, and the two cocks inside me started a slow matching rhythm, withdrawing when the other thrust in so I was completely and utterly filled. My magic was also enjoying itself from basically being tied down by Alec's magic, thirsty bitch, and it far too soon had me close to an orgasm. I sank my fingers into Alec's back and tried to focus enough to hold it back, but my plans were thwarted when Alec fisted my hair and pulled my head back to expose my neck.

"Don't you dare," he told me, thrusting extra hard inside me and making me howl. "Give us all of it. Come for us, Jaz. Right now."

I did. Dear, god, I did. My body shot off in climax, making me shake in their arms, their relentless fucking not letting up for one second. Alec's magic was doing something extra special to mine, because before I'd even finished coming, I felt ready to do it again. They fucked my next orgasm out of me, and I was screaming loudly enough that everyone else in the entire dorm was sure to have heard it.

Gilbert's cold finger on my chin had me opening my eyes, just barely able to keep them from closing again with so much pleasure running over me. He had his cock in his ghostly hand and was furiously jerking it off at the sight of me being fucked. "Again," he ordered. Alec's magic twisted and slipped into mine, making me come so hard I felt something stream out of me. Gilbert's magic joined ours, and though it was literally a ghostly touch, it felt exactly like having two cocks inside me at once.

My magic and I were equally full to the brim.

I climaxed again, and it didn't stop. It was wave after wave, never ending pleasure, I almost felt like I was going to pass out. Thankfully, I stayed conscious, and felt Alec come inside me moments before Pierce did. Gilbert shot his load over me and our magic receded, finally letting my orgasm end.

We collapsed in a heap on the mattress with even Gilbert in the fray, his cold arm across my back. The feeling of his hand on me was gone without Gilbert moving, and he groaned in disappointment. We'd had much more interaction than before, so that was something.

"I love you," Gilbert whispered to me, his smile warming my chest all over.

I was just able to kiss him before I drifted off to sleep, feeling more loved than I ever had before.

12

THE L WORD

I snorted awake some hours later with a sex hangover. Everything felt a little sore, but I was floating on a cloud and barely noticed.

As I took account of the men beside me and noticed Gilbert wasn't in the room anymore, I pulled the nightgown over my head and tossed it on the floor, just to be sure there wouldn't be a round two before I'd fully recovered.

Sliding off the bed, my legs were still wobbly as I walked to the bathroom and poked my head in to see where my ghost had gone. "Gil?" Something squeaked on the counter, and my little Merlin poked his orange head out from my shirt. I immediately went to him and made sure he was okay before going back out to where Alec and Pierce still lay on the bed. "Gil?" I called again and checked the rest of the apartment, only to find nothing.

When I went back to the bedroom, Alec groggily lifted his head and scrubbed at his face with one hand. He had major bed head, but he had never looked more attractive to me. "What's the matter, darling?" he asked sleepily, climbing off the bed. He stood and stretched, giving me a nice view of his naked body. Pierce stirred as well, his long hair in his face when he pushed himself up.

"Gilbert is gone," I told him, my voice shaking, and Alec came to me, only slightly stumbling with his jellied legs, and he wrapped me in a hug that warmed and comforted me.

"He'll be back," Alec assured me, smoothing my tangled hair over my bare shoulders. I knew that. I knew he just needed to recharge, but I didn't like it. I didn't like him not being with me. Standing up on my tip toes, I rested my chin on Alec's shoulder and curled my arms around him.

Gilbert made me feel wanted. Pierce made me feel loved. Alec made me feel safe. I needed all of those things, but especially Alec. No matter what happened, I knew I was just a hug away from feeling like nothing could hurt me.

I loved him.

I opened my mouth to say the words when someone's phone started ringing. Pierce wordlessly got up and went to retrieve it from his pants that were lying on the floor. He swore after reading the text he'd gotten, and I was curious what kept grabbing his attention like that. It definitely couldn't be another girl, soulmates and all, but I was definitely a little jealous, just in case.

He met my eyes and looked away. "Damn it." I almost asked the obvious question of *'what's up'* when he sat down on the bed. "I won't keep this from you guys anymore. I've been keeping contact with my pack."

Alec mock gasped. "*Shocking*. I knew."

Pierce dropped his shirt onto the floor and sat on the bed when I didn't say anything. "I've been careful, I'm not meeting with them, and they still don't know about you. I intend to keep it that way. I won't contact them anymore, just to be sure. I won't risk your safety."

"And you're fine with that?" I asked him, and he fixed me with an intensity that made me shiver.

"You're my family now."

I shivered again, and I wanted to hold him to me forever.

Without a word, Alec went to the dresser and brought out some jeans and a shirt that he placed beside Pierce on the bed. "Here's some fresh clothes. We should go shopping and get you more, but these will work for now. You'll have to roll up the legs, I expect." My warlock approached me, perusing my naked body with a heated look, and he tenderly kissed my lips. "I'll make some coffee."

Best soulmate ever.

I turned back to Pierce, and he crooked a finger at me. I slowly approach him, his heated gaze trained on me, and I straddled his lap on the bed. I brushed some of his long hair out of his eyes, pressing into him with a gasp when he gripped my ass using both hands.

"The perfect way to start my day: you naked in my lap," he remarked in a husky tone.

"Mmm," I mused, hovering over him and rocking my hips forward to rub against his erection. "I think the only thing needed to make it even better is you putting your cock inside me."

He clenched his teeth together and kneaded my ass like dough. "I stand corrected. The perfect way to start my day is you naked in my lap with my dick inside you." He crashed our lips together, stealing my breath away with his intensity, and letting me go before I was finished kissing him. "I can smell how wet you are for me," he whispered against my lips, and when I moaned long and low, he reached a hand between us to my sensitive folds, delicately running his fingers around my clitoris. "I know I promised I wouldn't say it, but…" He brushed some of my hair back, his heated expression the same one he'd been giving me throughout the week. I knew what it meant, and I finally felt ready to hear it.

Pierce leaned down for a sweet kiss with a quick flick on my clit. "I love you, Jaz."

My heart was about to burst. I'd never wanted to hear those words more, despite my reluctance before now. He had clearly expected me to complain about such a declaration, but instead, I raised myself up and guided his cock inside me. Being that I was indeed extremely wet, he had no trouble going all the way in, so deep I gasped and had to steady myself against him. When I'd caught my breath, I hungrily kissed him and tilted his chin up to stare into his brown eyes.

"I love you, Pierce."

There. I said it. For the first time in my entire life, I said those words to someone that wasn't my parents. And I meant them with every fiber of my being.

I loved Pierce and his adorable face. I loved his jokes, his smile, the way he looked at me like nothing else mattered to him. I loved spending time with him, laughing with him. I couldn't imagine my life without him.

I loved him.

With those words exchanged between us for the first time, Pierce's desire melted into pure love as he looked up at me. "I know I just said it, but *god*, I love you. I love you so fucking much." He held my face close to his and thrust into me, slowly raking against my walls as he withdrew and pushed back in.

I'd never felt so alive before that moment in Pierce's arms, and after letting my feelings loose, I knew he wasn't the only one of them that I loved. I loved all three of my men. The first chance I got, I was going to tell Alec and Gilbert how much I loved them, but first, *Christ*, I just wanted Pierce to keep fucking me.

His slow and deep pace usually would've made me impatient, but it felt too good to complain. Every thrust sent a burst of pleasure through me, adding to the slow building wave within. It steadily went higher, just drifting me along with no end in sight.

He was doing it on purpose, drawing out my pleasure until I went mad with impatience. I surfaced from the gentle pleasure and didn't want to go back under.

I wanted to come.

Pierce could tell when I'd decided this, but he kept with his slow grinding pace, that furry bastard. My eyes rolled back, and I let out a long groan of frustration that he drank up like milk.

Slow thrust, slow withdraw. He raked along my walls, my body still yearning for more, and I whimpered despite myself.

"I should do this more often," he teased with another agonizingly slow thrust. "Seeing you straining like that, desperate to come. I'd make you beg, but I know you won't."

How right you were, Pierce. Although at that precise moment, I was close to doing so.

He fisted my hair, lifting me up in his lap. "Alec is watching." A shiver went through me, and Pierce didn't allow me to turn my head to see. "I told you I would show him how I can make you come."

He hadn't done that last night?

All thought was erased when Pierce started fucking me. I mean pounding into me, breathlessly, forcefully, claiming my body as his. I was frozen in place, not knowing where one moan ended and another began, and that slow drift towards climax became a speeding car that picked me up and slammed me into a wall until I was screaming and coming for Pierce.

My legs shook, my body was flying apart, and my throat went hoarse before I collapsed on him. He was equally out of breath, having climaxed somewhere in the middle of my orgasm, and he flopped back onto the bed with me on top of him.

"Tasty," Alec commented from the doorway, the smell of coffee drifting to my nose. I couldn't move to see him, but the coffee scent came closer, and he appeared on the side of the bed where my head was facing. Still stark naked, he sipped from a mug, maintaining fierce eye contact with me. I was so distracted, I almost didn't notice the second cup in his other hand. "I leave you two alone for one minute and you slow fuck her to death. We are seriously going to get noise complaints. Mind you, I don't give a flying fuck, but it would probably mean a trip to Cauldron's office."

"And that's different from your normal schedule how?" I asked, sitting up with Pierce's softened cock still inside me.

Alec snorted into his drink and handed me the other mug. "Fair enough."

My coffee was strong and sweet, just like I liked my men. Well. Strong, commanding, and then sweet. It chased away my sleepiness and I felt more awake.

Pierce just lay beneath me as I sipped away at my coffee, gently holding my hips. Every so often, I wiggled against him and his cock twitched inside me. I liked having him underneath me like that. Maybe I'd have to try it again, but with him completely immobile. I'd control when and how he came.

"You're thinking evil thoughts, aren't you?" he asked, and I didn't answer, just tipped my mug over my face to drink the last bit of my bean juice. I handed the cup back to Alec and slowly crawled up Pierce's body until his cock slipped out of me, and I booped him on the nose.

"You'll find out."

I climbed off the bed and went to the dresser, picking out some clothes knowing full well they were getting an eyeful of my bare ass. Turning, I looked down at Alec's cock that was standing at half-mast. "Need me to help with that?"

"I would take you up on it, but I already took care of that while I was watching you come." I stalked over to him and stared into his eyes as I took a single finger, swirled it around the slippery head of his cock, and brought that finger to my lips. "*Jesus fucking Santa in a hat.*" Putting my hand on his neck, I pulled him down and kissed him, letting him taste himself on my tongue. He looked momentarily stunned when I let him go. "*For cauldron's sake*, I'm going to die from my cock being hard all day."

Pierce piped in from the bed. "Join the club. Not that I'm complaining."

Alec reached for me, but I slipped out of his grasp and he grunted in disappointment. "Tease."

"You love it," I reminded him, and left for the bathroom. Merlin was waiting for me, squeaking happily when I rubbed his head. I showered and put on a purple dress, slipping Merlin into my bra, then I went to the kitchen.

Alec was in front of the stove and Pierce was at the sink. Sadly both of them were fully clothed, but I appreciated the nice view of their butts. I resisted the urge to smack both of them, just to see their cheeks bounce. Ahh, hell, I was going to anyway. I sneaked over to

Pierce and squeezed his ass cheek, making him slowly turn to raise an eyebrow at me.

"I'd say I'm surprised, but…"

"You definitely shouldn't be," I finished for him, and reached my other hand out to grab Alec's ass, who didn't even pause with what he was doing. Astella, his pink fairy armadillo, poked her head out from his shirt collar. As if sensing her, Merlin appeared between my boobs, and they cutely squeaked at each other.

Turning, Alec set Astella on the floor by his feet and gently plucked Merlin from my boobs to set beside her. They sniffed at each other and I felt Merlin's interest in her. He cuddled up against her, his small body half her size. I'd never seen the familiars of soulmates interacting with each other, but I hoped they would become friends.

"Astella likes him," Alec said with a smile as he picked up the pan he'd been cooking in and turned the burner off. "She doesn't speak with words, and she prefers only communicating with me, but she likes him. Not in a, '*let me have your weird primate children,*' kind of way. Friendship. But also, almost like he's her baby. She wants to protect him, like I want to protect you."

I went to the couch and got one of the decorative pillows, using a spell to make it more like a pet bed, and I put it next to the table, gently placing both animals inside it.

I like the pink girl, Merlin said, and Alec chuckled when he heard it.

With Astella watching over my little orange boy, I eagerly sat down to eat the breakfast Alec had cooked us: pancakes with whipped cream.

"I had no idea you could cook, by the way. You're going to spoil us."

He served me up several pancakes and carefully spooned the cream on top. "Nonsense. You deserve every bit of it."

"So," Pierce started with his mouth full. "It's Saturday. What's on the agenda?" He was eyeing me hungrily, giving me the distinct impression that he wanted to spend the day in bed, and I was right there with him.

"I'm afraid I need to go to the library," Alec answered, looking like he was going to get blood drawn instead of merely *reading books.* "Still working on my project. I'd have you help, Pierce, but you need to stay with Jaz and protect her."

Speaking of books, I definitely needed to explore that necromancy book again and find someone who could translate it. Cauldron had promised to be my mentor, and there was no one better to ask. So, no day in bed. Damn.

"I've got something to do as well. And yes, Pierce will be with me, protecting, all that fun stuff."

Alec looked skeptical, but he let it slide and quickly

finished his food. He put his dishes in the sink, kissed my head, retrieved Astella, put his shoes on, and he was gone.

Pierce scraped a bit of whipped cream from his plate and licked it off while staring into my eyes, making my stomach jump at the thought of him licking it off my body. "We're doing something dangerous, aren't we?"

Dangerous for your stamina if you don't fucking *stop that*.

"Not yet."

"Well," he said, gathering up more cream and reaching over to slide his finger in my mouth, just to watch me lick it off. "When the time comes, I will be there to protect you, as promised. Alec can suck a dick."

"Don't tempt him," I said around the cream. "I will tell him if it comes up, I promise."

Pierce nodded and got up, taking our dishes to the sink where the enchanted sponge started cleaning them. Putting Merlin in my bra, I got my bag and we put on our shoes. Pierce interrupted me by shoving me against the wall and kissing me until I was out of breath and I'd dropped my shoes on the floor.

"Just to tide us over until I can hold you again," he said against my lips, and he shifted back to his giant silvery wolf form, sitting like a good boy and waiting for me to finish putting my shoes on. He cutely wagged his giant tail, sweeping the floor with it.

Bending just slightly to be level with his head, I tugged on his Ouija board pointer necklace and kissed his wet nose, then I hugged him close and buried my head in his soft fur.

"I love you," I whispered to him.

He sneezed on me.

13

THE PACK ARRIVES

Wolf Pierce followed me out of the soulmate dorm, but I didn't want to find Cauldron just yet. The forest beside Highborn was calling to me. Weird, I know. A bunch of fucking trees being like, *hey baby, come over*. Rolling my eyes, I left the school grounds and went down the hill to the forest.

As soon as we were inside the tree line, Pierce shifted back into a human and grabbed my hand. "I'd say we shouldn't be here, but you already know that. If *anything* comes close, you run back to the school, got it?"

"Even us?"

I jumped back when someone's voice came from deeper in the forest, and Pierce pulled me behind him as faces started appearing from behind the trees.

"*Fuck me*," Pierce ground out. "It's my pack."

Fuck me.

Pierce's pack slowly, warily, made their way towards us, as if the tiny pink haired witch was as much threat as a grenade. Half of them were in human form, the other still large wolves, though none were as massive as Pierce's wolf form.

At the head of the group was a tall girl whose face resembled my Lycan mate. Their eyes were the same.

"*Oppa*," she hissed when she reached him. She let out a string of words in Korean, and I really wished I knew what she was saying. It better not have been about my shoes.

Pierce hastily answered back, clearly not happy to see her, before turning to me with a hesitant smile. "Jaz, this is my sister, Gia. Gia, this is my mate, Jaz." Gia looked me up and down, a snarl marring her perfectly sculpted face. She spoke more in Korean and Pierce snapped at her. "*Hey*," he reprimanded sharply. "English, Gia."

Gia visibly wilted under her Alpha's command, and she frowned, sulking as much as possible. "*Oppa*, you can't be with this witch," she ground out. "You know what happened when *Unni* dated a fae. *Omma* was furious." She shuddered at the thought of it while I contemplated pulling my phone from my pocket to look up the words they were using, because if Gia was calling him

Oppa, it definitely didn't mean what Pierce had said it did.

Pierce grunted out a word that quieted his sister, and addressed me before I could say what he knew was coming. "*Oppa* means older brother. *Omma* is mother. *Unni* is older sister."

"You said that *Oppa* meant *boyfriend*," I accused with a squint.

"It means both," Gia clarified, still with a pinched look in my direction.

"I am not calling you that, Pierce. Nope. Forget it. Also, how many sisters do you have?"

"Five."

Oh my god. Just the thought of what their bathroom probably looked like had me cringing. Six women in one house, that was a disaster waiting to happen.

"Two are older, three are younger," he continued. "The older ones have their own packs, all of my sisters are Alphas like me. Gia will have her own as well."

"Sooner rather than later," Gia said as she crossed her arms over her chest. "I'm not sticking around with witch trash, no matter what she is to you, *Oppa*."

"Okay, whoa," I stopped her with my hand out. "Rude much?"

Gia growled loudly, snapping her jaw at me, and it caught me so off-guard that I visibly flinched and took a step back. Pierce answered her with a roar that shook the forest, making all of the wolves flinch back exactly as I had. With them cowering, his arms came around me and he held me close.

"I won't let anyone hurt you," he whispered to me, and I caught Gia's murderous look over his shoulder, not all of which was directed at me. He let me go, keeping me close still, and addressed his pack. "Gia is your Alpha now. You don't have to follow me anymore. I know what I've done is something you consider unforgivable, but you know as well as I do that we don't have a choice who our mate is."

"I would rather die than touch wizard *scum*," Gia ground out, and *Jesus Christ*, she needed to chill the fuck out.

Pierce stayed cool under her ire. "Fine. That's you, Gia. I chose differently. You don't have to see me ever again. Tell *Omma* whatever you want. Now go before someone from the witch school sees you."

Even with her hating him, he still looked out for his sister. She clearly didn't appreciate it because she rudely wiped her shoe on the forest floor and whirled her finger around to signal the pack to leave. They all walked past us, spitting, flipping us off, or saying something about my mom being a whore.

Gia was last, and she gleefully sneered at Pierce. "I'm going to tell *Omma* and *Appa* the truth. And when they know that you're sleeping with the enemy, *Appa* will end you." She didn't appear to care about saying that to her own brother, and I wasn't about to let it stand.

Before he could stop me, I stepped in front of Pierce and raised a warning finger to my future sister-in-law. "You listen up, you little skank. If you ever speak to Pierce like that again, I will rearrange your idiotic face, and I don't need magic to *beat your ass*."

She turned her nose up at me and sneered again. "As if."

"*Bitch!*" I shouted, and Pierce grabbed me around my waist to hold me back as Gia took off running into the forest, shifting into a small red wolf before she disappeared. I wiggled away from Pierce and grunted angrily. "That *fucking...*"

His face stopped me short. He was watching the forest in the direction they'd all left, and a single tear fell from his eye down to his cheek. He hadn't just lost his pack. He'd just lost his entire family. His friends. His *life*.

All of that was because of me.

With more tears falling down his cheeks, I wanted to hold him in my arms and make them go away, but I wasn't sure if he wanted me to, since again, this was my fault. He turned away from the forest and settled on me, giving me a sickening guilt in my stomach, but that melted away when he held out his hand to me.

I raced to him and he met me in the middle, his arms clutching me so tightly it hurt, but even when he loosened his grip, the pain in my chest didn't go away. I clutched him to me with my arms around his neck. "I don't want this for you," I said hoarsely through my own set of tears.

He breathed in and tried not to let out a sob. Just the thought of him crying had me crying even harder. "It's okay. This was going to be the outcome since the moment we met. I knew it. I've accepted it."

"Your sister is a cunt," I responded with a sniff.

He laughed brokenly and ran his fingers through my curls, to comfort himself as much as me. "She was never pleasant." I felt him looking up over my shoulder, still searching where they'd gone. "I..." He sighed and rested his chin on me. "I hoped someone would come back." The forest remained silent, drawing another deep sigh from him. "I'm not sad that they left me. I'm sad that their hatred was that deep. People say that they love you, but they only love you when you behave the way they want. The second you deviate from their expectations, they don't want you anymore."

"I want you." I knew saying that wasn't the same as hearing it from his sisters, from his parents, his friends. But I needed him to know that I meant it, because the pain he was feeling was more than I could bear. "I will always want you."

He relaxed against me. "And I will always want you." We stood in that embrace for a few minutes until he had stopped crying. "I know what I said to Gia was a little callous."

I didn't remember anything he'd said as being callous. He'd been far more polite than I had. "Say what?"

"I said that we don't have a choice who our mate is. It's true, I won't deny that. But whoever that person is, they're always someone we would've chosen for ourselves. I would choose you out of a crowd of pink haired weirdos any day."

"So romantic," I cooed sarcastically, loosening our hug, and he gave me a weak smile. His beautiful face was streaked with tears and he had some phlegm on the tip of his nose. I wiped it off with a smile. "Do you want to meet my parents?"

He laughed, spewing me with tears. "You want me to meet your parents? Won't they hate me?"

I gave a half-shrug and brushed his long bangs from his eyes. "My biological dad was my mom's *magicae equidem*. She, more than anyone, knows what it means to have a soulmate. I don't expect her to instantly invite you over for tea, but…"

"She won't disown you for it."

I pressed my hands to his chest and shook my head. "I don't think she would. Granted, she's an elemental witch who sets shit on fire when she's seriously pissed off, and she's super annoying most of the time. So, you know, fifty-fifty shot." I curled my fingers on his shirt. "I can't... live with you losing everything because of me. So, I'm going to give you everything that I have. It won't fix it, but maybe it will help." I'd intended to say more but he cut me off with a deep kiss, one that lasted forever, but still wasn't long enough.

"I didn't lose everything," he said against my lips. "You're still here."

"So sappy," I squeaked, and almost felt like crying again.

"We should get back to school and do that thing you needed to get done."

"No, I need to hug... you..." I pulled away from him, and that calling was back. "Uhh, babe. Is there something dead nearby? I feel weird and that's probably what it is, since I definitely can't have two familiars."

"This is a forest. Animals die in here all the time." I gave him a blank stare and he rolled his eyes. "Okay, sorry. Anything for you." He shifted into a wolf and sniffed around, finding scents that were beyond my nose to catch, and he took off running.

"*I have stubby legs, you bastard!*" I shouted as I ran after him. I was deeply winded by the time I found him, and he was sitting in wolf form, happily wagging his tail for me.

Beside him was a dead rabbit, not unlike the one I'd resurrected at the High Council test. This one was pure onyx, and there was a thin layer of dirt on its fur. I sat down beside it, just staring at the pile of fluff. Pierce shifted back again and scooted to sit next to me.

"What do you think? This it?"

It was. The calling was still there, centered in on the rabbit.

He leaned his head against my shoulder and rubbed his hand across my back. "You don't have to do anything."

"I know."

"You can just leave it here."

"I know."

Merlin poked his head out of my shirt and stared down at the rabbit.

Rabbit is dead.

"Hey, you're getting better at talking, little guy," Pierce praised, and Merlin let him rub his tiny head.

Mommy fix the rabbit?

With a tiny tarsier asking you in baby talk if you'll fix a rabbit, saying no made me feel like a dick.

"I'm not ready."

Merlin accepted that, trying not to pout so I wouldn't feel bad. My excuse was simply that, an excuse. I was ready, I just didn't want to fail again.

Pierce got up and took his coat off, then gently picked up the rabbit with it, covering it with the jacket.

I resisted asking the obvious question of, *'what are*

you doing,' mostly because I genuinely was confused *why* he was picking up a dead bunny and putting it in his coat.

He saw my questioning look and pointed to the jacket. "We're taking it back to the apartment. You felt a pull to it, so I'm assuming there's a reason. Whenever you're ready, you can resurrect it."

"Attempt."

"Attempt," he repeated with an annoyed look in my direction. "I'll get Alec to put a spell on it so it won't decay or smell bad, so there's no pressure on you to hurry up. Okay?"

"Okay," I weakly agreed.

We took it to our apartment and left it on the couch with a note in case Alec got back before we did, then we left again and walked to the main school building for our real destination: all the way up to the floor where Cauldron's office was. My legs were hurting before we'd even gotten halfway there, and I let out a string of swear words over how much I hated stairs. Pierce licked my hand to help me feel better, so I pat his head and limped down the hallway.

Cauldron's door opened when I knocked on it, allowing us to enter his super dark and extremely filthy office.

"Heyo!" I shouted to the darkness. "You here, Headmaster?" It was lit only by a few candles, but I still craned around to see Cauldron's short frame amongst the mess. I definitely needed to sit before we'd gotten confirmation he was even in there. My weak legs were about to give way after the stair abuse, so I cleared off one of the low tables and sat on it.

"Jaz, lovely to see you again," the headmaster's voice finally called from somewhere in his cave. "What can I help you with?"

"I'm afraid it's something of a... sensitive matter."

"Do tell," he said with interest, and I heard some rustling, but he still didn't appear.

"Okay, can I turn on a lamp or something? It's creepy as fuck in here."

Then again, with the lights on, I'd be able to see exactly how many dust particles I was inhaling. *Gross.*

His snap echoed through the room, and a few lights came on, illuminating the space enough where I could at least see everything, and *holy fuck,* how many stacks of books does one person need? He put my grandmother to shame, and she never put her fucking books back.

Also, there was enough dust in here to create a *colony* of dust bunnies. And I was right about seeing the dust particles before they went up my nose. Oh god, I'm never breathing again.

Cauldron appeared, and thank Christ, he was holding a bottle of wine and two glasses, as he usually did.

"Apologies about…" He gestured with his short arm at, well, *everything* in the room, since it was now all visible.

"Don't care, wine please." He poured me a glass and I eagerly took it, gulping the red liquid down like it was water. "Ahh," I exclaimed with a happy sigh. "I love visiting you. You have the best wine."

"That's not why you came." I gave him my '*duh*' face and held my glass out for more wine. He obliged before pouring his own and sitting in one of the low stools next to the table I was on top of. "First things first, how are your studies coming?"

"Well…" I smacked my lips and licked away some red droplets. "I talked to that demon again." Pierce's ears perked up, and he let out a short gruff that probably meant, '*YOU WHAT?*'

Cauldron had a similar reaction, but he hid it by drinking from his glass. "I presume you had a reason."

"I needed his opinion on whether or not I should continue resurrecting. He's the most unbiased person I could ask, since he definitely doesn't like what I am."

"And?"

I swirled my wine around before taking a sip. "He said that my bleeding heart meant that I was taking my powers seriously. And that was good." Saying it out loud made me realize how true it was. Or maybe I was just tipsy already. "That's *also* not why I'm here." I took my coffin bag off my shoulders and dug around in it with one hand until I found the necromancy book, and I handed it to the Headmaster before taking a large gulp of wine.

He turned it over in his hands and shifted his eyes up at me. "Safe to open?"

I nodded and flipped back some of my curls. "Alec made sure." Cauldron sipped his drink, perusing through the book, stopping at some pages and skipping others. "We weren't sure what language it was."

"It's fae," he noted, still flipping through.

Fae. If we could find one of them to translate it, maybe they would also help me find the right magic to search for Gilbert's body.

Cauldron was marveling over the book like it was a dirty magazine. "I've never seen a spellbook in a beast language before. Utterly fascinating. And this belonged to the former necromancer, whoever came before you?"

"That's what they told me," I answered without thinking. God damn, I didn't even have the excuse of being drunk.

"They?"

I groaned into my glass and it echoed. "I met with a necromancer cult. Well. *Met* probably isn't the right word. They kidnapped me."

"*What?*" I flinched and hoped he wouldn't throw the book at me. "Who kidnapped you, describe them."

"Umm... Satyr. Chick dating satyr. Lycan. Other

weirdos. There was a throne."

Cauldron seemed content with my answer, though I couldn't say why it mattered. "Lucky for you, I know a fae that might be willing to translate this. Fae are slightly neutral in the war, so it won't be a problem for us to visit."

"My question is," I began, and was just starting to feel a nice buzz from the wine, so I drank more of it. "Why didn't the cult translate it before? They've had it for a while, obviously. But no translate?"

"They didn't need to. No one could use the spells."

Mmm. That made sense.

Merlin squeaked and I reached a finger in my bra to scratch his head. "Shush, Merlin."

"Merlin?" Cauldron asked with raised eyebrows. "I thought the wolf's name was Pierce."

"*Sure*." I got up and finished my second glass off. "Can we go to the fae right now? Alec will be super duper pissed if I'm not there when he gets back from the library. *Fuck*. I wasn't supposed to tell anyone. He's embarrassed."

"His secret is safe with me." Cauldron stood and held the book up for me to take, then he disappeared behind a pile of books. I was almost worried he wouldn't reappear again, but he was back by the time I'd tucked the book back into my coffin bag and slung it over my shoulders. "Let's go, Miss Neck."

14

A FAE DEAL

The silence in Cauldron's car was both awkward as fuck, and a total blessing in disguise. I was buzzed, and I didn't have to talk at all. I could've used more wine, but hey, the day wasn't over yet. Pierce had opted for basically sitting *on* me instead of going to the back seat, and his tail swished against Cauldron's short legs whenever I looked down at him.

I had to do something special for Pierce. He'd just lost his family over me, and I meant it when I said I'd give him everything I had. Basically all I had was my coffin backpack and a bunch of witty comebacks, but I still wanted to think of something.

Busy contemplating what I could do, including a

house warming party with my parents so they could meet everyone, I stroked Pierce's fur and watched morning turn into afternoon outside the car windows. We'd been in the self-driving car for at least an hour before it left the main road and went off to an unpaved path.

"Hey, Headmaster," I said, breaking the silence as we drove through a forest. "This friend of yours is cool, right? He won't, like, kidnap us or whatever?"

Cauldron didn't immediately answer, which was worse than his actual response. "Not with me here. You have nothing to worry about." Pierce's ears perked up and I knew he'd have something to retort back if he could speak. Or he just needed to pee. I know I did.

The trees opened up to a small clearing with a *creepy ass* house in the middle. And when I say creepy, I mean imagine the Beast from Beauty and the Beast was actually Jeffrey Dahmer, and this was his house. Sure, it was a gorgeous old structure with charm, but that charm promised only awkward looks and inappropriate questions.

Cauldron's car parked itself in front of the creepy house and we got out. I bent my head back to take everything in, from the towers to the weird glow in one of the windows. Merlin sensed my unease and popped out between my boobs. I tried to shove him back into my bra before Cauldron saw him, not to mention I also didn't want the Headmaster staring at my chest.

"What was that?"

Fuck. He saw.

"Uhh... a Pokémon?"

Cauldron sighed at me and turned his attention to Pierce. "Since we're not at school anymore, I think we can dispense with the pretense. I know that this is a Lycan."

"*What!* Outlandish!" I snapped, sputtering over my words as my stomach plummeted. *God damn it,* Aurora was right.

The Headmaster rolled his eyes at me. "Calm down, Miss Neck. Alec's masking spell is very good, but I knew the instant I saw him. If I haven't told anyone by now, you can assume I will keep your secret."

Pierce was shifted back to his human form before I could stop him, and he skeptically stared down at Cauldron who appeared completely casual about all of this. "We can assume? That's super comforting."

"How do you think you're able to still go in and out of the barrier? And what did you think it meant when you were assigned one of the bigger soulmate apartments? If I wanted you gone, I wouldn't be accommodating you." He paused, looking back at me. "And to just make sure I understand the situation, you're his mate, yes?"

I nodded and took Pierce's hand. "I won't be parted from him. Even if I have to leave school."

"I'm sure I don't have to explain that you're not only risking his life, but yours and Alec's as well. If you're found harboring a Lycan, you could be tried for treason."

"As could you," Pierce added, and Cauldron chuckled at him.

"Fair enough. I'm Wolfgang Cauldron. I'm sure you've heard my name, but let's be properly introduced." He held out his small hand and Pierce gently shook it.

"Pierce Kim." He pulled his phone from his pocket and quickly texted someone. Was it his pack? "So, should I shift back before we go inside?"

"No, the fae will see through Alec's glamour, but you should stay out here, just to be safe."

Pierce nodded and quickly pulled me to him with an arm around my waist, taking me a few feet back so we had some privacy. "You're about to go somewhere that may not be safe, and I can't go with you. I know you don't like taking orders, Jaz, but you will stay by Wolfgang's side, you will not wander off. If I have to come find you again after someone has taken you or you've run off, I will be very cross with you. There will be no excuses for disobeying me. I don't care if you have to pee, you will not be out of his sight." He bent to grab me around the waist and hoisted me up in his arms, my feet dangling in the air, and I embraced him back. "I cannot lose you, Jaz," he whispered, his voice wobbling just enough that my chest squeezed. I clutched the back of his head with my hand and stroked his long hair.

"She'll be fine, Pierce," Cauldron offered gently as he watched us.

"We don't take chances with her," Pierce explained, and I burrowed my head in his neck to hide my blush. His behavior was starting to be endearing instead of annoying. Dear god, I was smitten.

Goddess, if I change from surly to sappy, I will be super pissed.

He continued clutching me to him as the minutes passed, and I sighed heavily, going limp in his arms. "You know, this was cute at first, but now I would like to be able to breathe," I commented, my voice muffled by Pierce's jacket.

"Breathing is overrated." I rolled my eyes and grunted my disapproval. He finally set me down and kissed me until I felt dizzy, then he pressed a finger to my nose. "No wandering off."

"Fine. Bossy." I slowly kissed him, loving the way he smelled and tasted. "I love you."

He brushed some of my hair back and pressed his lips to my forehead. "I love you."

Pierce reluctantly let go of my hand and I walked

with Cauldron to the front door of the giant house. He knocked on the middle part of the wood, anxiously tapping his fingers against his leg as we waited, and then the door opened.

I'm not really sure what I was expecting, mostly because I had no idea what the fae looked like, but the guy standing in the doorway had me raising my eyebrows. He was *wickedly* hot with grey-blue skin and long silver hair. He was lean and tall like a bean stalk, but he also had a weirdness to him that made me feel like he was a creepy uncle. A creepy uncle with abs that were chiseled from *stone, god damn.*

My vagina was very confused.

"Calllllllldron," he drew out, and I had the distinct impression he was as high as a kite in outer space. Or he was just a weirdo. When he noticed me standing there, his expression changed, and I had that creepy uncle feeling again. "And friend." He held out a hand for me and I reluctantly gave him mine, only for him to plant a kiss on my palm. "*Enchanté.*"

Pierce, now would be a perfect time to get jealous and attack his nuts.

"Please, come in." The fae stepped back, thrusting his hand out to guide us into his house. His front room was a nice parlor, almost too nice, like any second the furniture would jump out and eat you. The creepier part wasn't that no part of the room looked like someone actually lived here, it was that everything perfectly matched the fae's grey-blue skin.

While I was observing this, my back prickled, and I turned to see him looming over me.

"I'm Sebastian." His nostrils flared and he slowly looked down at my mouth, tilting his head at it like my lips were interesting. "You are mated." He could tell that from my mouth? "Perhaps your mates would allow a fourth lover in your bed."

Fourth? How did he know I already had three?

Also, yeah, *that will happen*.

"Sebastian, please. Not my students."

The fae straightened with a slight pout and flipped his silver hair back. "Wolfgang, what brings you to my humble abode? Would you like any refreshments while we chat?"

"No, we would not," Cauldron said quickly. "Never eat in a fae's home, Jaz."

"Mmmmm," Sebastian purred at me with delight. "Your Headmaster is correct. If you do, you can only leave with our permission. And I do so hate to give permission for my friends to leave."

"*God*, you're still creepy," Cauldron muttered under his breath. It was nice to know he was feeling it too.

The fae pursed his lips in amusement and

approached a small bar to pour himself a glass of vodka. I tried not to stare at it with too much longing. "Well, then. Will you please answer my question?"

Cauldron patted his leg and it started jingling. "I have a bag of coins in my pocket. You can have it if you will translate a spellbook for us. It's written in fae."

Sebastian hummed to himself in a laugh. "So specific with your words, as always. Words matter, young necromancer. Speak one incorrect word, and you have no idea what will happen."

I needed Alec.

Swallowing hard, I tried to picture him by my side so I wouldn't feel so vulnerable.

Cauldron raised his hand to me and I produced the spellbook, bending to hand it to him. He gave it to Sebastian, who thumbed through it while sipping his drink. His amusement was rising higher as he quickly scanned the pages, and he'd finished his drink by the time he got to the end.

"It's not a spellbook, this is a journal," he pronounced, setting his glass down on the bar. "Written by a necromancer, but I'm sure you knew that. It's dated four hundred years ago, just around the time of the last known necromancer. From what I can gather, that necromancer was rather naughty. I'm sad we never met."

"We'd still like it translated, please." Cauldron pulled

out a little pouch from his pocket and placed it on the bar beside Sebastian. "For your troubles."

Sebastian purred again and poured himself more vodka. "Shouldn't take me too long, and you can come pick it up once it's done."

"We'll be on our way, then. Thank you, Sebastian. Jaz, let's go." Cauldron put his hand on my hip and was practically pushing me towards the door as the fae smiled at me.

Even with his creepy eyes staring at me, I couldn't waste this opportunity, because I knew I probably wouldn't get another one. "I need something from you," I told him quickly.

Cauldron groaned and shut his eyes in disappointment while Sebastian's cute face intensified.

"Remember, little necromancer. I told you words matter. Do not ask for something that you cannot afford."

"Jaz, please be quiet," Cauldron hissed.

"I need to find a corpse."

The fae raised an eyebrow at me, taking a sip of his drink. "Weird flex, but okay. And you need bone magic to do this, of which I can provide." His demeanor changed from creepy kitten to creepy lion as he studied me over the rim of his glass. "And what can you provide in exchange?"

"*Jaz*," Cauldron cautioned again, and I waved a hand

for him to be quiet, but he ignored me. "You never start a deal with a fae without first making it very clear what you will pay them."

"I'm sorry, did you offer a crash course on fae deals before we went inside? I'm flying blind here."

"Unfortunately, it's too late for assistance," Sebastian told me, and he put his glass down on the bar. "You have told me what you want, we just need to negotiate the price."

"I *swear to god*, if you say my firstborn, I will junk punch you."

He snorted and crossed his arms over his chest. "Babies are annoying, I'd rather have lunch with a troll." Contemplating his choices, Sebastian's stare made a shudder run up my spine, but was even worse when he smiled creepily at me. "I'll have a kiss. That will be my price. A soulmate level kiss." He held out his hands and puckered his lips.

My vagina was no longer confused.

"Can we circle back to the firstborn option again?"

"I'm afraid not, little one. Once I decide on my price, you can either pay or leave. I suggest pay, but I am biased because I will enjoy a kiss from you, even if I may lose my penis after your soulmates find out."

True dat.

Sighing, and trying not to shudder again, I wiped my

mouth across my arm and shook my hands to relieve the tension.

It was just a kiss. Just a kiss with the creepy fae.

I could do this.

I approached the grey-blue skinned fae and pointed a warning finger at him. "You touch my boobs, and I will personally remove your dick. No need to worry about anyone else doing it."

"Noted," he purred, and that *totally didn't help you twat bag*.

I closed my eyes and I pictured Gilbert. My sweet ghost with his shaggy brown hair and his beautiful eyes. I liked to imagine they were green when he was alive, it seemed to suit him. I reached my hands out to the person in front of me, and it was Gilbert's soft, loving fingers that I felt. Fingers that were warm and real, just like I wanted him to be.

His thumb ran along my jawline and he cupped my neck, tilting my head up so he could bend over me. Our heated breath mixed for a few moments before I closed the distance between us and captured his lips in mine.

I could've wept at the feeling of Gilbert in my arms, tangible and alive. I pressed our bodies together and curved against him, kissing him long and slow, savoring every touch of his lips. He slipped his tongue into my mouth and I gasped, pulling him closer to me with my hands on his shirt. I was up on my tip toes, and I still had to tug him down to me for more kisses. Kisses I didn't want to end.

The man in my arms gently untangled me from him and set me back on my feet. I opened my eyes again, remembering where I was, and that Gilbert wasn't here. He hadn't been in my arms, kissing me exactly the way I wanted him to.

I could've wept, but I held it together. Just barely.

Sebastian was silent, and though I barely knew him, it didn't seem to be his normal behavior to not comment after something like that. He lifted his hand and hesitated before gliding his thumb along my cheek and tucking a curl behind my ear, that small action making a shiver run through my body.

Dropping his hand, he turned to the bar and opened a drawer, rummaging for a bit before he found what he was looking for. He turned back to me and reached for my arm, holding my hand out, and putting a tiny marble on my palm.

"As promised." I would've made a comment about it being a *marble*, but my voice had been stolen from me. "I apologize. I did not realize your love for your mates was so deep. If I had a woman who kissed me like that every day, I would never suffer another man to touch her." The fae stepped away from me, as if he needed to put distance between us. "The marble will need a high level enchantment using the blood of your target's *magicae equidem*, but it will find your corpse."

I swallowed and curled my hand around the marble. "Thanks." I put it in my pocket, turning to leave when I heard something outside, and my heart leapt out of my chest.

Pierce.

15

THE WOLVES DESCEND

I raced outside to see Gia's pack had arrived and were gathered around Pierce. She still had that snooty look on her face that intensified when she saw me. I pushed through their ranks, all of them avoiding touching me as if I had cooties, until I reached the center where Pierce stood.

"Get out of here, *witch*," Gia ground out, her eyes trained on her brother in case he moved.

"I asked you not to speak to her like that." Pierce's voice was dangerously low, his steadiness more unsettling than if he'd yelled at her. It even made *me* afraid, and I knew he would never hurt me. I was more worried about him attacking his sister, because that would definitely make family reunions awkward.

"I told them," she announced with hateful glee, and Pierce just barely flinched beside me. "*Appa* has never sounded so angry before. I hope you're happy, Pierce. You brought this on yourself."

Goddess, I really want to kick my future sister-in-law right in the tit.

Gia bared her teeth at Pierce, and more people appeared from the forest, another wolf pack. My Lycan lost his control for a single second when he saw who they were. This pack had older wolves, and at the head were two perfect specimens that I accurately guessed were his parents.

His dad was a *daddy*, make no mistake. Stacked, s.t.a.c.k.e.d. with muscles. He was twice as big as his son, and Pierce might've been short, but he wasn't a small dude. Mr. Kim had a lush beard and short black curls that looked as soft as Pierce's hair. It was a shame I had to hate him for being a complete prick to his son.

His mom was drop dead *gorgeous*. She might've been slender in frame, but she had muscles out the ass. She looked like she could beat someone up with one finger. Her long black hair was tied up in a French braid.

At their sides were two girls that looked like older versions of Gia, and another two that were younger versions of her.

We had the entire Kim family here, everybody. Not

the best way to meet your boyfriend's parents, but hey, nothing is perfect.

Stupidly, and literally knowing it wouldn't do anything to help should it come to it, I came forward and stood in front of Pierce to shield him from his bitch parents.

"Hello Mr. and Mrs. Kim. I'm your son's disgusting girlfriend, Jaz Neck. It's very nice to meet you. I take it you're not interested in coming over for Thanksgiving dinner?"

Mr. Kim gave me a quick threatening glare that had me gulping. "Shut up."

"Rude," I whispered, and Pierce tugged me back behind him, which was definitely a good idea considering his mom was giving me the '*I will cut you*' face. She was way scarier than Daddy Kim.

"I had to come see for myself if what Gia told us was true," Mr. Kim said. Gia's pack parted for her parents to approach us, and she respectfully bowed her head to their father, the head Alpha. Mrs. Kim had her eyes trained on me, and her hands were balled into fists. "I hoped she was lying. I'm very disappointed to see she wasn't."

One of the sisters definitely looked disappointed as her mouth soured at Pierce. "How could you, Pierce? You had everything, and you threw it away for *that*." She gestured at me like I was a pile of horse turds.

"*I didn't have a choice*," Pierce ground out, reaching back to take my hand. "If the same thing happened to you, what would you have done?"

Gia spit on the ground, a trend with her, it seemed. "I would've killed myself."

Mrs. Kim's eyebrows rose at her daughter's brashness, and she hid it when she saw me watching her. "You're coming home with us, Pierce. I know you'll die without her, so we'll let you see her once a month. You'll survive with that. And no one will ever know."

My mouth popped open in disbelief that they would even consider that, but Pierce was already shaking his head.

"Absolutely not, I will never leave her. We've mated, it's done. I won't survive a week without her now, and you know it." All of Pierce's sisters rolled their eyes like he was being dramatic.

"You will not stay with this *whore*," Mr. Kim bellowed. "You are a worthless son. You have always been worthless, and you will die worthless."

Clenching my fists, I could feel my powers rising in tune with my anger. I can forgive being called a whore, but calling Pierce worthless? Absolutely not.

"*How dare you!*" I ground out, my magic bursting around me in pure rage, exactly the way my mother's did when she got pissed.

Mr. Kim growled in response, but if he was trying to scare me, it wasn't going to work this time. "You will not speak to me like that, witch."

"*And you won't speak to my mate like that!*" I lifted my hands and everything in that clearing that wasn't tied down shot into the air. Rocks, twigs, leaves, all hovering around us in a swirling tornado, waiting for my anger to peak.

It was very clear with the general look of shock that went around the pack that they had underestimated me.

Good.

Mr. Kim slowly stalked closer to his son, the tension between them thick and unsettling, and my hands shook from the effort of holding everything up. "Let's settle this, Pierce."

If they fought, one of them wouldn't be coming back up.

"Jaz!" someone shouted, and I caught sight of Alec and Gilbert approaching from the driveway.

The sight of them set the wolves off, and several things happened at once.

A giant black blur appeared at the side of my vision, and I turned to see what it was as Gia launched herself at me. The black blur was a wolf, I couldn't tell who. Pierce broke the stare off with his dad when he saw Gia coming towards me, and the black wolf used that opportunity to attack, claws and fangs ready to tear Pierce apart.

Before the black wolf could close his jaw around Pierce, the blur of Alec's body flew to protect him, and he took the attack instead. Wolf Gia was on me before I could see what had happened, sinking her teeth into my shoulder and ripping my skin. I lost control over the rocks and branches, which came crashing down over us. Gia wrenched at my flesh, and I cried out in pain, but Pierce was there to throw her off me.

I barely felt the pain in my shoulder as Pierce helped me up. My thoughts were consumed with Alec, and I saw him over Pierce's shoulder, lying motionless on the ground. Pierce let out a hoarse shriek, but my voice was gone as I crawled across the dirt to Alec's side. With the amount of blood coming from Alec's neck, I didn't need to be a necromancer to know my warlock wasn't going to make it.

Goddess, don't do this to me again.
Please.

I was frozen. Frozen in fear. Everything I'd been afraid of was happening. I was losing someone I loved again.

"Alec, *no*," Pierce cried out as he hovered over Alec. The warlock's bloodied throat constricted, and he weakly held out his hand for me. I fell on my knees beside him and took it. Pierce had Alec's other hand held between his own like a vice. "*Why Alec?*"

My warlock smiled through the pain as best he could. "You're my family, Pierce. I will always protect you." He turned to me and gave another smile, tightening his fingers around mine. I could hardly see for the tears in my eyes. "I love you, Jaz. I should've told you sooner, I'm so sorry, darling. You don't have to say it back, I know you will someday."

My heart splintered off into a thousand pieces as his declaration loomed over me. Even now with him dying, he wasn't willing to push me further than I was comfortable with.

I smoothed his hair back, a tear falling from my cheek to his, and I bent over to give him a gentle kiss. "I love you, Alec."

"*Called it*," he whispered, and with a contented smile, he closed his eyes and his chest stopped moving.

༄༅༅

IT FELT LIKE IT HAD BEFORE, SITTING OVER THE BODY of someone I loved. I felt lost. Broken. Alone. Only, when I found my father's body, it didn't feel like this. This felt worse.

I felt hollow, like a husk. There was nothing left

inside me. Nothing without Alec. This was what my mother felt every day. I had no idea. No idea it would hurt this much.

I knew it would destroy me, but I didn't know it would *destroy me*.

I didn't think, I acted. I wrenched off my backpack, tearing one of the straps as I did and ripping the zipper seam. It didn't even register to me, I just pulled things out of my bag that I needed.

Peeking out from my shirt, Merlin was silent, but it was a silence I heard as if he'd spoken. He was trying not to feel anything so he wouldn't make it worse.

Where pink girl?

"Pierce," I got out, just barely able to speak through the perpetual stream of tears that continued falling down my face, ones I didn't bother wiping away. "Find Astella." He got to it, checking Alec's pockets for the little armadillo, and I practically emptied my bag to get all that I needed. Taking stock, I knew I was short a few things, and I didn't know what to do if I couldn't get them.

As if I'd summoned him, Sebastian appeared with a handful of herbs, candles, and whatnot. Cauldron was beside him, holding up his wand to the Lycans in warning.

"It's time for everyone to leave. You've done enough here."

The wolves moved away from us, retreating back into the forest, all except for Pierce's mom whose worried expression made me want to scream at her.

"Can you bring him back?" she asked me, watching me hovering over Alec.

"Why do you care?" I ground out as I sorted everything. Pierce said something to her in Korean and she left without another word.

On a whim, I got out my mortar and pestle, grinding up some herbs from my bag and stealing a few that Sebastian had brought. I didn't care if he wanted something for them, I'd worry about it when Alec was alive again.

Once the herbs were ground into a fine powder and their potent scent was wafting up to my wet nose, I stared down at them and got the distinct impression I should spit into the bowl. Why? No idea. I did so, and stirred them around with my pestle, and that part felt right. Gross, but right.

Merlin squealed and I looked up to see Pierce had found Astella. She had some blood on her, but she was okay. I took her from him and slid her into my bra too. She was almost too big to fit, but she was glad to be near me. For the first time, I felt her in my head, and that was the feeling she gave. She was sad, but she trusted me to bring Alec back.

I got out my chalk and I started drawing a circle

around him, the runes and lines so much more intricate than any I'd done before then. When I leaned up on my heels to inspect them, I knew something was off about it, but I didn't know how to fix it.

"Darling," someone said above me, and my head instantly shot up, but it was only Gilbert. I hadn't conjured Alec's spirit back yet. "I might have a suggestion. Maybe something in the circle about healing his wounds?"

I looked back down at my work and realized he was right, that's exactly what it was missing. I amended here and there, still not understanding anything that I was writing, but it started to feel right.

Now it was time to call his spirit.

I looked up at the night sky and pictured Alec's steel eyes. "Alec, come back to me."

"I told you I would never leave you," he said, instantly appearing above me, and I breathed a sigh of relief, even though my heart was still aching. "And here I am, in all my ghostly glory." He looked about the same, only he had Gilbert's silvery hue and was transparent. His smirk still made my stomach jump, ghost or no.

"Welcome to the spirit realm," Gilbert greeted as he glided up to Alec, and they shared a small fist bump.

I let out a shaky laugh. "If this doesn't work, I'll have two ghost boyfriends."

Alec smiled down at me. "All I ask is that you try, my love. Whether it's today, or a year from now, you will bring me back. I have complete confidence in you."

I wish I did too.

It didn't matter, I was going to try.

I took the bowl of herbs with my spit mixed in, placing it on Alec's chest, something I hadn't done before. I arranged my candles in various spots around him and straightened to look everything over. It all seemed fine. Perfect? I wasn't sure. But I felt enough confidence to give it a go.

Goddess, if you never do anything for me my entire life, do me this one solid. Help me bring Alec back.

Hoping that would work, I looked up at Alec, and he lowered himself down until his ghost self hovered over his mortal body. "Ready?" He nodded, I raised my hands, and I started speaking the incantation. The words took a life of their own as they poured out of me, spinning out and around us until everything was twirling and rushing.

My power strained against me. I'd drawn almost all of it out, and it was so hard to control, I didn't know if I'd be able to.

Out popped Merlin from between my boobs with Astella beside him. They connected to me, and somehow a chaotic burst became a thin controlled line.

Most of it was Merlin's doing, but Astella added what she could, and both were pleased to have aided me.

Grinning with confidence, I reached out for Alec, and he took my hand. His was cold, but it felt solid and real. We stared into each other's eyes for one final look, I chanted the spell one last time, and I slammed his spirit back into his body.

We waited for what felt like an eternity. Waiting was torture. The seconds felt like eons.

And then…

Alec sprang to life, gasping in a breath, and he sat up, tossing the bowl of spit herbs off his chest.

"*Bloody hell.*"

Pierce fell into Alec for a hug. Cauldron was there to check on him and praised me for doing so well. Even Sebastian was impressed. Gilbert joined the Alec hug, and my three men held out their arms to me, inviting me to join them.

But I stood frozen, waiting with dread that was threatening to overturn my stomach. Waiting to see if Alec would stay alive.

I waited.

And waited.

And waited.

End of book two

Book Three in the Neck-Romancer Series
Neck-Rophiliac

ABOUT THE AUTHOR

Photo by Elizabeth Dunlap

Elizabeth Dunlap is the author of several fantasy books, including the Born Vampire series. She's never wanted to be anything else in her life, except maybe a vampire.

You can find her online at
www.elizabethdunlap.com

facebook.com/edunlapnifty
twitter.com/edunlapnifty
instagram.com/edunlapnifty
goodreads.com/Elizabeth_Dunlap
bookbub.com/authors/elizabeth-dunlap
amazon.com/author/ElizabethDunlap
tiktok.com/edunlapnifty

OTHER BOOKS BY ELIZABETH DUNLAP

Born Vampire Series

<u>Teen edition (15+), Adult edition (18+)</u>

Knight of the Hunted

Child of the Outcast

War of the Chosen

Neck-Romancer Series

Neck-Romancer

Neck-Rological

Neck-Rophiliac

Highborn Asylum Series

Freak: A Highborn Asylum Prequel

Visit her author website at

elizabethdunlap.com for more titles